Praise for *Get Carter*

"Aristotle, when he defined tragedy, mandated that a tragic hero must fall from a great height, but Aristotle never imagined the kind of roadside motels James M. Cain could conjure up or saw the smokestacks rise in the Northern English industrial hell of Ted Lewis's *Get Carter*."
—**Dennis Lehane, author of *Live by Night***

"Lewis was one of the first British writers in the sixties to take Chandler literally—" The crime story tips violence out of its vase on the shelf and pours it back into the street where it belongs"— and [*Get Carter*] is a book that I and plenty of other people at the time considered to be a classic on these grounds."
—**Derek Raymond, author of the Factory Novels**

"*Get Carter* remains among the great crime novels, a lean, muscular portrait of a man stumbling along the hard edge— toward redemption. Ted Lewis cuts to the bone."
—**James Sallis, author of *Drive***

"The finest British crime novel I've ever read."
—**David Peace, author of *Red or Dead***

"Ted Lewis is one of the most influential crime novelists Britain has ever produced, and his shadow falls on all noir fiction, whether on page or screen, created on these isles since his passing. I wouldn't be the writer I am without Ted Lewis. It's time the world rediscovered him."
—**Stuart Neville, author of *The Ghosts of Belfast***

"The finest British crime novel ever written."
—**John Williams, author of The Cardiff Trilogy**

JACK CARTER'S LAW

JACK CARTER'S LAW

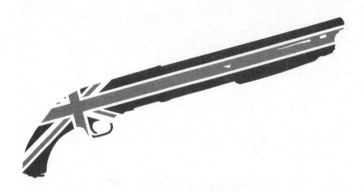

TED LEWIS

SYNDICATE BOOKS
NEW YORK

First published in Great Britain in 1970
by Michael Joseph Ltd.

This edition published in 2014 by
Syndicate Books
www.syndicatebooks.com

Distributed by
Soho Press, Inc.
853 Broadway
New York, NY 10003

"The Law, Crime and Ted Lewis" © Max Allan Collins

Library of Congress Cataloging-in-Publication Data
is available.

ISBN 978-1-61695-505-2
eISBN 978-1-61695-506-9

Interior design by Jeff Wong

Printed in the United States of America

10 9 8 7 6 5 4 3 2 1

THE LAW, CRIME AND TED LEWIS

an introduction by Max Allan Collins

The crime of Ted Lewis, of course, is that he is not well-known, either here in the USA and in his native UK. He's somewhat better known in the latter due largely to the high regard in which director Mike Hodges's 1971 film *Get Carter* is held (the movie is based on Lewis's 1969 novel *Jack's Return Home*—published by Syndicate Books as *Get Carter*)—in 2004, a survey of film critics by *Total Film* magazine lauded it as the greatest British film of all time.

Still, even in the UK, Lewis novels have been tough to find for decades. As a longtime fan, I'm hopeful that the republication of his three Jack Carter novels will lead the rest of Lewis's books back into print. While I'm no expert on UK crime fiction, I am not surprised that many critics across the pond consider Lewis the father—and *Jack's Return Home* the foundation—of a grittier school of British *noir* fiction.

What little has been written of Lewis's life indicates a man of considerable talent and suicidal impulses, not unlike his most famous character. Jack Carter is a cool-eyed professional whose risk-taking is at odds with his unflappable demeanor and the "law" that his philosophy of life seems to imply. He is neither sadist nor misogynist, but he kills without compunction and is happy to slap a female around if he thinks she needs shutting up. The uncompromising nature of Kray-era mob enforcer Carter mirrors that of Lewis the artist. Neither man does anything designed to particularly ingratiate himself with civilians.

That may be why the Carter follow-up novels—the UK paperbacks utilizing the familiar Michael Caine imagery—were his most successful post-*Get Carter* publications, though some knowledgeable critics consider his long out-of-print final work, *GBH* (Grievous Bodily Harm), his finest novel. By any reckoning, Carter represents Lewis's single popular success.

Like Carter, Lewis was handsome, a womanizer, a heavy drinker, and a thumber-of-the nose at authority. He paid for all of that with a short life—like Carter—but both men made their mark. If life were fair—and I'll pause to light up a fag while you laugh your arse off—Lewis would be as famous as Carter has become (thanks to Mike Hodges, Michael Caine, and smart UK critics).

Like most American fans of Lewis, I met Carter in the film version and then went seeking the source novel, for which there was a movie tie-in paperback bearing the *Get Carter* title. In 1971 I was heavily under the influence of Donald E. Westlake's Parker novels (which he had written as Richard Stark). And I had met Parker in the John Boorman directed/Lee Marvin-starring *Point Blank* (1967), based on another crime novel whose original title (*The Hunter*) was supplanted by a more famous film adaptation's. Movie reviews at the time considered *Get Carter* a British take on *Point Blank*, and that was certainly how I viewed it. Both are great films, but *Get Carter* is clearly the nastier, the grittier, the more uncompromising of the pair.

At around age twelve, I had discovered hardboiled crime fiction—the term *noir* still just a gleam in the eyes of various French film critics—and began with Dashiell Hammett, Raymond Chandler and Mickey Spillane, in part because their private-eye progeny were all over American television screens in the late '50s and early '60s. Lewis apparently began as a Chandler fan himself—an enthusiasm referenced by Michael Caine reading *Farewell, My Lovely* on the train in *Get Carter*—and he has at times been termed "the British Mickey Spillane." (More about that later.)

Soon I was reading novels with criminal protagonists, written by James M. Cain, W.R. Burnett, Horace McCoy, Jim Thompson and a slew of forgotten paperback writers. Still, that early infatuation with private eyes sent me as a young writer in that more heroic direction, which, as the '60s darkened into the Vietnam War, began to seem more and more naive and even quaint. But Richard Stark's Parker pointed in a new direction—it seemed a revelation that a professional thief, in the anti-establishment late '60s and early '70s, could fill the same kind of heroic role as Chandler's Philip Marlowe or Spillane's Mike Hammer. How much of a stretch was it? After all, Hammer had been a brutal avenger who dealt with bad guys in their same homicidal terms.

Not that it's important, but whether *Get Carter* (film or book) influenced the creation of my hitman character Quarry is something I just can't remember. I think I'd already created Quarry by the time I saw *Get Carter*, but maybe not. Meaning no disrespect to Donald E. Westlake, I know I had begun to think that, for all their toughness, the Parker novels hinged on an inherent cop-out by the writer—Parker himself never killed civilians and had no truck with accomplices who did. Also, the Stark novels were told in a skillful third-person—with a strict use of point of view—that created distance from the reader. Protected the reader.

I decided that Quarry would be a hit man, not just a thief, and that the stories would be told in the first-person. In the opening chapter of *Quarry* (1975), the lead character murders a priest—it was my way of telling readers,

"Now's your opportunity to get off the bus." I can't say how Quarry compares to Jack Carter—both are very much men of their home countries—but as written by Lewis, Carter makes Parker look like Rebecca of Sunnybrook Farm.

The Carter novels are not only told in the first person but in present tense, usually an unbearable approach but, in the hands of an artistic craftsman like Lewis, a dazzling way to keep the action in the now, all while staying invisible as a technique. Carter is not only unapologetic about his activities and attitude, it never occurs to him an apology might be necessary. He is that rare character—one that we quickly understand but who remains able to surprise us at every turn. Oddly, he often surprises us as much by those he chooses not to kill as by those he does.

Jack Carter's Law is not for the faint-hearted crime fiction aficionado, and for the American fan, the experience can be challenging, as Lewis immerses us not only in the milieu of the London underworld of the late '60s, but in its pungent slang as well. I have a hunch that even readers in the UK might need some help here. But like any good writer using slang that might be unfamiliar, Lewis is careful to provide context that will show the way. It doesn't take long, for example, to realize "the Filth" are the police.

In *Get Carter/Jack's Return Home*, the protagonist is operating as a kind of unlicensed private eye, very much a Mike Hammer type seeking revenge over the murder of his brother. That element of shared humanity—who among us doesn't understand the desire to avenge a murdered friend or sibling?—gives the first Carter novel an aspect of protagonist justification that makes the uncomfortable experience more palatable. It's a mystery novel, after all— we're looking for a murderer, and he or she will be brought to rough justice. (Just *how* rough, we would never have imagined.)

But in the prequel *Jack Carter's Law*, the mob enforcer has nothing remotely noble in mind. His job is to find a squealer and kill him, and his motivation is to keep himself and his bosses out of jail. In this way, *Jack Carter's Law* is even tougher and more uncompromising than its famous predecessor. And perhaps it's why no prequel film came about from it, and why the two later Carter novels were only modestly successful.

Still, it's also an indication that those two follow-up novels were not just fast-buck affairs—nothing at all pandering is to be found in their pages. Lewis was too crafty an artist to give his audience a free ride. But he gives them a ride, all right, and a wild one, the only shock absorber that deadpan understatement from the narrator himself.

As gritty as Lewis is in *Jack Carter's Law,* he still reveals the influence of Chandler, although Lewis doesn't strain for poetry in the way that Chandler sometimes can (and that all of his imitators do). Lewis finds the simile that doesn't seem unlikely coming from a hard man's mouth, as when he describes the drawing of curtains making "a noise like paper money," and when he describes a gay joint as smelling "like the inside of a handbag." Not that poetry is absent in Lewis, who points out that "scraps of cloud race across a cold-glowing moon."

The Spillane influence is here as well, and for all the American critics (then and now) who like to diss and dismiss Mickey, his impact was felt enormously throughout crime fiction in the '50s and '60s, and not just in America. Spillane was the most widely translated author of his day and was particularly popular in Great Britain—he liked to say they translated him into English (referencing words like "center" becoming "centre" and "color" becoming "colour").

The grittiness of Carter's underworld—stale smoky bars and glittering ganglord's pads and grungy underlings' flats—is as vivid and surreal as the New York of 1950s Spillane. And Lewis describes all of this in mesmerizing detail, painting scenes with care and in no hurry. Elmore Leonard was a crime fiction writer of understandable renown, but his famous "rules of writing" includes: "Don't go into great detail describing places and things." This clearly does not apply to Lewis.

Consider this: "The only lighting in the hall apart from the rectangles above the billiard tables comes from behind the counter, illuminating the Kit Kats and Mars Bars and the cellophane of the cigarette packets beneath the dirty glass of the display cases." That's just one sentence in a long paragraph that puts you inside the Premier Social and Sporting Club in a way screenwriter Leonard never could, or at least didn't bother to.

The most overt Spillane influence has nothing to do with tough guys or murder mystery—it's the breakneck manner in which Lewis describes action, pulling the reader in and down into a breathless captivity marked by long sentences and scant punctuation, where run-on sentences and the over-use of "and" are something the copy editor will just have to fucking live with.

But Spillane's fever-dream Manhattan is never as real as Lewis's London, and while Hammer is a good guy who defeats bad guys with their own methods, Carter is simply a bad guy with methods. Neither Hammer nor Parker would lose any sleep over killing him. So why do we care about him?

We're back to Lewis, the craftsman, the artist, who knows that locking us inside Carter's first-person narration means we'll early on decide whether or not to take the ride. Lewis also knows that as bad a man as Carter is, he remains the best man in his world—which is the real secret behind writing a story about a criminal protagonist. The people around Carter are even worse than he is. Like Stark's Parker, Lewis's Carter is a professional and not gratuitously mean. Even when he hits a woman, Jack only gives what is needed at the time to complete the job.

Along those lines, you'll in these pages meet a compelling and even tragic character, Lesley, who demonstrates Carter's complicated take on how a woman with information should be handled. When Lesley's mistreated, he saves her; when she misbehaves, he slaps her; when someone else gives her more rough stuff than seems deserved to Carter, somebody might get killed over it. You may have guessed that political correctness is not an issue in Carter's world or Lewis's fiction.

In the end, Lewis is his own man, quirkily, defiantly so. Whatever he may owe to Chandler and Spillane, however he and Jack Carter may be compared to Richard Stark and Parker, no one can honestly say that anyone else ever wrote books like these before, which perhaps explains why Lewis is considered a cult favorite. Westlake—often termed such himself— once said, "Being a cult favorite is three readers short of the writer making a living." Lewis, like Jim Thompson, did not live to see his work widely appreciated and applauded. But like Thompson, Lewis deserves discovery and major reevaluation.

What is Jack Carter's law? Well, the title only *seems* to refer to the Old Bill (police), even if the American title of the book was *Jack Carter and the Law*. Carter's law, filtered through his own off-kilter hooded-gazed point of view, is the law of the underworld, where a "grass" is a betrayer who must be coldly cut down, just as the killer of your brother must meet your fiery rage.

MAX ALLAN COLLINS is the author of the Shamus-winning Nathan Heller historical thrillers (*Ask Not*) and the graphic novel *Road to Perdition*, basis for the Academy Award-winning film. His innovative '70s series, Quarry, has been revived by Hard Case Crime (*Quarry's Choice*) and he has completed eight posthumous Mickey Spillane novels (*King of the Weeds*).

JACK CARTER'S LAW

Cross

THE PARKED ROVER SHUDDERS and sways in the wet wind that races down Plender Street. Plender Street is empty and lifeless except for the toffee papers and the newspapers and the fag packets that now and then are caught up in the swirling drizzle that's slapping away against the steamy windows and deserted landings of the flats.

I look at my watch. Cross is late by forty minutes. Jesus, I could have been tucked up between clean sheets humping Audrey by now. As it is I might not even have the time, not with Gerald and Les breathing down my neck to find out what's going on.

I look in the driving mirror and there's a taxi coming round the corner, making spray like a corporation water cart. After it comes out of its drift the driver points it at the rear end of the Rover so I get out and walk to the back of the car. The taxi pulls in to the curb and the door opens and I get in. The taxi begins to move again.

"So where the fucking hell have you been?" I ask Cross, and he says, "It's silly being like that, Jack. You know that. I mean, you ought to by now."

"Don't shoot shit at me," I tell him. "You've never been late before."

And he says, "No, but there's never been a situation like this before, has there?"

"I don't know," I tell him. "You tell me. That's what we pay you for."

The cab smells of old cigarette ends and Cross's damp raincoat. I pull the window down slightly and Cross takes his hands out of his coat pockets and places them in his lap and examines his fingernails like all the cheap B-feature coppers do. I take out my cigarettes and my lighter and Cross's eyelashes flicker when he realises that I'm not producing the envelope. He can wait, like I've had to.

The cab crosses Camden High Street and I light my cigarette and as I light it I look at my watch and wonder how long Audrey could risk waiting for me at the flat.

"All right, let's be having it," I say to Cross and Cross reaches up and takes hold of the passenger strap and looks out of the window and says, "Well, for a start, nobody knows where he is."

"What are you talking about, nobody knows where he is? He was taken into West End Central three days ago. Mallory goes to see him two hours after he's been picked up and he goes to see him again yesterday for the appearance. Then Swann goes down again to await Her Majesty's Pleasure. So what the fuck are you talking about?"

"What I'm talking about is that Swann never went back whence he came," Cross says. "As far as I can discover he never even left Bow Street. He did, of course, but nobody saw him go. And as nobody saw him go, well . . . "

Cross leans forward and taps on the partition and slides back the glass and says to the driver, "Turn round and stop on the other side of the road."

The driver does as he's told. Now it's my turn to look out of the window. The rolling slope of Primrose Hill swings into view and beyond it the smudgy city shimmers through the steamy window. The cab stops and rain sweeps against its bodywork.

"I've asked everyone that can be asked," Cross says, "and nobody knows a dickybird."

"And so what do you think?"

Cross allows himself a faint grin. "Approximately the same as you," he says.

When I don't say anything Cross says, "Well, there you are."

Then he leans forward and slides open the partition again and tells the driver to take us back to Plender Street.

On the way Cross says, "If, for one reason or another, this turns out to be the last time we meet on a professional basis, I'd just like to be able to think that when you remember all the little favours I've done you and Gerald and Les, then you'll forget you ever heard my name or saw my face."

I put my hand in my inside pocket and take out the envelope and put it against Cross's mouth and push upwards, causing the envelope to buckle against the underside of his nose, forcing his head back onto the shelf behind the seat.

"Listen, cunt," I tell him, "what's in this envelope is all you get in return for your favours. And just remember this: I'm not so stupid that I don't tumble you're just telling me half of what you know, like you always do. So if there's a time when there's a few names flying this way and that don't forget that yours begins with the third letter of the alphabet."

The taxi draws up behind my Rover and Cross tries to get the envelope away from his face and says, "What I've told you is all I know."

"Oh yes? Well if there's anything you've overlooked then phone me or Gerald or Les before ten o'clock tonight. Now take your pigging money and let me get out."

I let go of the envelope and it falls in Cross's lap. While he's smoothing out the envelope I open the door and rain spits into the cab. I look at my watch. Sod Gerald and Les. They can wait for an hour. I slam the cab door behind me.

Audrey

I'M LYING BACK IN bed, smoking, and I say to Audrey who I've just lit up in more ways than one, "Isn't it about time you had your nails cut," and she says to me, "Leave off, you know that's one of the bits you enjoy best," and I must admit she's right, only of course I don't admit it to her. I take a few more drags and look down my body and at her body which is naked except for the half-slip which, time being of the essence, we never got round to taking off. The slip's all twisted up round her waist except for a little bit of lace edging that's overlapping the top few curls of her pubic hair. I reach down and pull the slip away so that she's all exposed and she gives me a look. "Do me a favour." I tell her, "Not yet, what do you think I am, James Bond?" She pulls a face. "All it is," I say, "is that it's a long time till your next visit to the hairdresser's, isn't it, and I like to remember," and she says, "Funny." At first I don't tumble and then when I do of course I have to laugh.

I finish the cigarette and get off the bed and walk over to the table where we'd left the vodka and ice and slices of lemon and I liven up my half-empty glass and ask Audrey if alcohol might not be an anticlimax after what we've just been through and she says, "What about you then?"

"I've got to steady my nerves down after that," I tell her and she says, "Well, you'd better give me one because I've got to steady mine down because I've got to phone Gerald. I'm late."

"I've got to phone him too," I tell her. "I should have been at the club an hour ago." I make her drink and take it over to the bed picking up the phone on the way. Audrey takes a drink but she doesn't touch the telephone, just stares at it, as she lies there propped up on her elbow. "Someone, somewhere wants a phone call from you," I say, but all I get for that is "Piss off." I shrug and take a drink and sit down on the edge of the bed. "You know what would happen, don't you," she says. I know what's coming but I don't say anything. "I mean," she says, "if Gerald ever got to know about us." "Yes, I know," I tell her. "We'd both be dead." "No," she says. "You'd be dead, you'd be the lucky one. What he'd do to me would be much more interesting. I mean, Gerald really enjoys going to work." "I know all about Gerald," I tell her, lighting up another cigarette. "You think I don't know about that?"

"I must be bleeding barmy," she says, and I tell her yes, she must be bleeding barmy. "I mean," she says, "doesn't it worry you?" "'Course it worries me," I tell her. "What do you think?" "Well, you never seem to," she says. "No, well . . . " I tell her. Then there's a long silence and after that she picks up the phone and dials the number. I lie back on the bed and rest my head on her stomach. You've got to give her credit for being a great little performer because when the receiver's lifted at the other end she delivers "Hello sweetheart," just the way she does whenever she phones me. I can hear Gerald's reply even from where I am. "What the fucking hell do you want?" he says. "Oh, bleeding charmin'," Audrey says, her hand over the receiver, "just bleeding charming." "Look," he says, "didn't I tell you I'm having a meeting all afternoon? Didn't I tell you that?" I transfer my cigarette to my other hand and reach up and start massaging Audrey's breasts. She tries to push my hand away but her being propped up on one arm and holding the receiver in her other hand she doesn't have much joy. I carry on with the therapy and she says, "Yes, I know, darling, but I had to phone and tell you why I'm going to be a little late because I know how you worry." "All right, let's have it," Gerald says. "So why are you going to be late?" I take hold of her arm and pull her forward so that she overbalances off her elbow and falls with her breasts resting on my lower stomach. She mouths silent rage at me but Gerald's voice rasps down the line and she has no time to recover her previous position. "The thing is," she says, "I ran into Yvonne in the hairdresser's and what with Harry just being sent down she wanted to talk, you know, so I'm back at hers now. God knows how I'll get away, you know what she's like . . . " "Fucking Harry," Gerald says. "A right bright bastard he is. Serves him bleeding right, don't it? I mean, going out with those fucking amateurs, fucking ponces . . . " Gerald stokes himself up on the subject of Harry and I slip my hand behind the back of her neck and push her head down until I can feel the warmth of her breath tickling the tip of my prick and the closeness of her breathing begins to take effect because she looks from it to me and her expression changes and a different kind of wickedness appears in her eyes and she lays the receiver on my belly, the mouthpiece against my prick-end, takes me in hand and begins to go to work, all the time looking into my eyes, and all the time Gerald's barking voice reverberating through the plastic against my skin. Eventually Gerald's voice stops and Audrey puts her mouth next to the mouthpiece, her lips brushing my tip, and she says, "I know, darling, you were right, you were always right about Harry, especially when you got rid of him. I mean, how could you trust a man who's stupid enough to trust those ponces, you could see it coming," and Gerald says, "Too fucking true, he was a berk." Audrey says, "Anyway, I'll be back as soon as I can. If I'm back too late tell Ann-Marie no later than seven with the kids, you know she spoils them," and Gerald says, "Right," and she says, "How about a kiss, then?" "For Christ's sake," Gerald says, "you know who I've got here?" "I'm not going to let you go without a kiss," she says. "Oh, all right," Gerald says and makes a kissing noise down the phone, and she fakes one back, only her lips, when she purses them, are kissing me, and like I say, not on my mouth. The line goes dead and she carries on with the kissing.

After Audrey's gone I have a shower and do myself a steak and salad. Gerald and Les can wait a bit longer. They're not to know what time I met Cross. While I'm eating my steak and having an extra couple of drinks I watch television but I really don't take anything in because I'm thinking of what Audrey said about being barmy carrying on together. I'd had that thought ever since we'd first tumbled. But the alternative, rowing out, just wasn't on as far as I was concerned. Not since that very first time. Every bird I've ever had was just so much cold meat compared to Audrey. And in any case, trying to row out from a bird like Audrey would be just as dangerous as the present situation. The shit would fly whatever I did. So as usual I give up thinking about it and put on my gear and start out for the club.

Gerald and Les

THE RAIN HAS STOPPED and the greasy streets are full of tourists trying to turn up the naughty bits of London. I get out of the cab and unlock the sober sage-green painted doors and Alex is standing there behind the lobby's glass doors, his teeth highlighted whiter than ever beyond the glass's bright reflection. I push open the glass doors and Alex helps me off with my coat.

"Anything?" I ask him.

"Nothing yet, Mr. Carter. A small game in the Green Room but it won't get any bigger. The rest are just drinking." Up above me there is the faint sound of Motown-style music.

"All the girls reported?"

"All of them," Alex says.

I walk over to the plain door next to the cloakroom and unlock the door and open it and slide back the cage doors of the private lift and press the button. The lift only has one stop and that's Gerald and Les's penthouse office on the top of the club. The lift smells like the inside of a stripper's G-string which isn't surprising considering the amount of slag traffic it's carried since my bosses, the Fletcher brothers, had it installed eighteen months ago.

You'd have thought Gerald would have had enough of slags considering the route by which the two of them arrived at the top of the building that was now the centre of their operation. But not Gerald. Slags to him are like scotch to an alcoholic. Not that Les is a total abstainer but more often than not he'll pour himself a drink and watch Gerald get on with it, with the kind of mild interest someone else would watch a couple of kittens at play. Les lives his life more in his head than Gerald does.

The lift stops and I get out. I'm in a small windowless hall. There is only one piece of furniture, a leatherette swivel armchair, and sitting in the armchair is Duggie Burnett. He's wearing a hound's-tooth suit—two buttons with side vents, narrow trousers with deep turn-ups—a yellow waistcoat, a Viyella check shirt and a plain woolen tie. He'd look like something straight off the early-morning downs at Newmarket if it wasn't for the fact that his nose is on sideways and the rings he wears on each of his fingers aren't there just for show. At the present moment he has a serviette tucked in his waistcoat and he is genteelly balancing a plate of sandwiches on his knees. The sandwiches have been daintily cut and served up with slices of tomato on top and a patterned doily underneath but Duggie is absorbed in gently taking the sandwiches apart and placing the salad stuff to one side and picking up the slices of ham with his fingers and eating them that way. Each time he places a slice in his mouth he thoroughly cleans the grease off his fingers with his handkerchief. I stand there watching him for a minute or two before I say anything to him.

"And supposing I was Wally Coleman and six hundred of the fellows that walk behind him?" I ask Duggie. "What would that make you and Gerald and Les by now?"

"But you ain't," says Duggie, not looking up from the disemboweled sandwiches. "If you was you'd be headfirst down that lift shaft with a bullet up your arse, no trouble."

I grin at him.

"All right," I say. "Let them know who's here."

He wipes his hands again and picks a handset off the wall next to him.

"Jack's here," he says, and puts the handset back on its cradle.

The door opposite the lift slides open and as I go in I say to Duggie, "Incidentally, it's on the news a gorilla got out of Regent's Park Zoo this afternoon. Haven't caught him yet. If I was you I'd stay at home tonight."

The door slides to behind me. I'm in another hall, bigger than the last. This hall has furniture, Regency repro, and gold-framed pictures, but there still aren't any windows. The hall is lit by a single light set dead centre in the ceiling. There is another door, a replica of the one that is the entrance to the club, painted the same colour. I press a button on the wall next to the door and a second or two later the door is opened by another mug called Tony Crawford, the only difference between him and Duggie being that Tony's gear is ten years out of date and that he'd eat the ham and the bread and the doily and the plate.

"Right, piss off, Tony, this is a meeting now," says Gerald.

Tony closes the door behind me.

The room I am in is all Swedish. It's a big room, low-ceilinged, and when Gerald and Les had it built on top of the club they'd let a little poof called Kieron Beck have his way with the soft furnishings. Everything about the room is dead right. The slightly sunken bit in the middle lined with low white leather settees with backs reaching the normal floor level, the honey-coloured polished floor itself with its scattered furs, the office area over by the window which runs all the length of one wall, the plain white desk that is worth half an Aston Martin, the curtains that make a noise like paper money when you draw them—everything is perfect. The only things that look out of place are Gerald and Les. So much so that they make the place look as if you could have picked all the stuff up at Maple's closing-down sale.

Gerald is sitting in the sunken bit, making the leather look scruffy. He is wearing a very expensive three-piece suit, gray chalk stripe, but with it he is wearing a cheap nylon shirt and a tie that looks as though he's nicked it off a rack in Woolworth's. His shoes are black and unpolished and one of the shoelaces is undone. But even if the shirt had been tailor-made from Turnbull & Asser and the tie had come from Italy and the shoes had been handmade at Annello & David he would still look a mess. One of those people that make a difference to the clothes instead of it being the other way round. Les, on the other hand, is immaculate. He is perched with his arse on the edge of the white desk, smoking a Sobranie. He's wearing one of his corduroy suits, the pale beige one, and with it he's got on a lavender shirt and a carefully knotted brown silk tie, a pair of off-white suède slip-ons and socks that match the colour of his tie. What is left of his hair is beautifully barbered, just curling slightly over the collar of his shirt.

Audrey is there as well.

She's over by the cocktail cabinet, getting the drinks together.

"So," says Gerald, "we're finally here at last, then."

I sit down on an armless easy chair in the raised-up part of the room. I don't say anything. There's no point until Gerald and Les have run through today's double act.

"I mean, we thought maybe Cross had nicked you or something."

Gerald laughs at the others, encouraging them to appreciate his wit.

"We thought he might have nicked you for being double-parked," Les says in his humourless voice.

Audrey gives Gerald and Les their drinks, then pretends to remember that I'm there and I just might want one as well.

"Do you want one, Jack?" she says.

Gerald laughs and says, "Do you want one, Jack? Eh, Audrey, why don't you give him one?"

He almost falls off the settee, he's laughing so hard.

"No thanks," I say to Audrey, looking her straight in the eye. "I had one before I came here."

Les frowns and says, "You dropped off for a drink before you came here?"

"That's right."

Les looks at Gerald and Gerald says to me, "Listen, you mug, we told you to come straight back here. What's the fucking idea?"

I look at Les and say, "Les, I left Cross three-quarters of an hour ago. After what he told me I didn't think a swift vodka and tonic would make all that much difference."

"Why?"

I take out my cigarettes and light up.

"Because," I tell them, "it's my opinion that Jimmy has been done good and proper and he's weighed up twenty-five years against appearing for the Queen. Against us. And various other past associates that we don't need to mention here."

Gerald stands up and begins to turn bright red. "Bollocks!" he says. "Bloody bollocks. Christ, what, with Finbow? Jesus, all Finbow has to do is pick up the phone and he's a few grand better off and Jimmy walks out a victim of circumstances. Besides, Jimmy'd never shop us. He's Jack the Lad. Jesus, Jimmy and me are like bleeding cousins. From way back."

"In any case," Les says as he lights a new cigarette from the end of his old one, "the cunt wouldn't dare."

"No," Gerald says. "He's right. The cunt wouldn't dare."

I shrug. There is a silence. Audrey crosses her legs and the nylons sound like static on a cheap transistor.

Les pushes his hands in the pockets of his jacket and the smoke from the cigarette in his mouth causes him to narrow his eyes and hold his head back so that he's squinting up at the ceiling.

"Is that what you really think?" he says.

"Well," I say, "look at it this way. Jimmy was at Norwood. He was at Walthamstow. He was at Ealing. He was at

Finsbury Park. Granted that wasn't one of ours but it's another job. He was at Luton and he was at Dulwich and we all know what happened there."

There is more silence and so I go on.

"At a rough calculation, I make it that Jimmy has done about a million and a half quids' worth of overtime for us over the last six or seven years. A real little cornerstone to the firm he's been. A right sweet little catch he'd make for some rising star in West End Central."

"Yes, but Jack," Gerald says, "it's Finbow, for fuck's sake. Herbert fucking Finbow."

"If it was Finbow that plucked Jimmy, he'd have phoned by now. And in any case Jimmy's been put out of the way. Finbow'd never do that. Unless Finbow's had the operation."

Gerald snorts. "Oh, yes, and I'm a fucking fairy."

I shrug again.

"Why don't we get in touch with Finbow and find out?" Les asks, as if I should have done it already.

"If it's Finbow, there's no point," I say wearily. "If it's not Finbow, there's still no point. Can't you see what I'm trying to say? Jimmy's being done proper. So whoever's doing him we can't get to. They're sticking it on him. And because they're sticking it on him they've made him some kind of offer so that it looks good for him to stick it on us."

"Yeah, but look," Gerald says, "supposing he gets offered fifteen instead of twenty-five. Christ, that's not big enough for him to drop in everybody else."

"You've got more faith in Jimmy Swann than his mother ever had," I tell Gerald.

Les gets up from the edge of the desk and walks over to the drinks cabinet.

"Anyhow," he says, "even if he took the ten years' difference he'd know we'd get him fixed on the inside. And Jimmy never was happy in a brace-up."

"Yes, that's right," Gerald says. "He wouldn't have the bleeding stomach for it."

"Unless," I tell them, "they're fixing it so nobody can get to him, ever."

"But why would they?" Gerald says. "What's the point? Christ, if Jimmy spills, half the population of Inner London'd be standing side by side in the fucking dock and half of Old Bill's mob as well. Jesus, they're under-strength as it is without putting their own boys away."

"We don't know what the point is, do we?" I say. "That's just it. We don't know what's going on."

"I thought that's what we paid Cross for," Les says, again looking at me as if I was to blame for Cross's lack of material.

"If Jimmy's turned Queen's evidence then Cross will be sending his information in the other direction from now on," I say.

After a while Gerald says, "If Jimmy's done a deal he must have given them something already."

"That's right."

"So if it's like you think it is then why hasn't anybody been picked up yet?"

I shrug. "Depends. If they want everybody Jimmy's worked with for the last half-dozen years, they want them all at once. They don't want anybody clearing out at the first arrest."

"But it still doesn't mean we can go on our holidays before we get to Jimmy," Les says, rattling the ice cubes in his drink. "And if you're right, then of course we've got to get to him, haven't you, Jack?"

I'm expecting that one so I say, "Sure. That's right. If you've got one of those diaries with tube maps on the back then I'll start right away. If I go through the alphabet I'll be at Wembly about 1980."

"We pay you," Gerald says. "You find him. I mean you haven't tried Finbow yet. Or Mallory. Christ, what about Mallory? Why the fuck hasn't he been in touch? It was yesterday. Bleeding yesterday."

I look at Les and Les looks at me. Gerald looks at both of us.

"What?" he says. So I have to spell it to him.

"If Mallory hasn't been in touch then he knows what's going on. So he won't exactly be sitting behind his desk waiting for us to get in touch with him."

Gerald stands up and walks a few paces then turns back and sits down again. His arse on the leather makes a noise like a bad diver hitting the surface of the water.

"So where are you going to start?" he says.

I shrug and get up.

"May as well start with the obvious," I say. "At least that way we'll make sure it's the way it looks."

Les downs his drink and says, "Maybe, but don't forget Swann's got to be found this week. Next week's too late. And when he's found, no mistakes."

I walk over to the door and open it and before I close it behind me I say to Les, "I don't make mistakes. Like, for instance, employing Jimmy Swann in the first place."

Walter

THE RINGING TONE WHIRRS in my ear for a long time before the receiver is lifted at the other end. There is no greeting so I say, "My name is Eamonn Andrews and this is your life."

There is a sigh of relief and Tommy says, "It's always nice to hear your voice on this number, Jack."

"Seeing as I'm the only one who has that number."

"Something like that."

I shake a cigarette from my pocket and say, "You doing anything tonight?"

"Yeah, I was taking the old lady down Ernie's."

"Not any more you're not."

"Why's that?"

"Because you're going to look for Jimmy Swann before he coughs so big you'll never be taking your old lady down Ernie's or nowhere again."

There is a long silence. Tommy knows better than Gerald and Les to worry his head about whether I'm wrong or not so he says to me, "What do you want?"

"I want you to talk to some of Jimmy's crowd and I want at least one of them to have something interesting to say to you. If you want some extra muscle get hold of Mickey and Del but make sure they're sweetened up. The less that gets around the better."

"I won't need them," Tommy says. "This kind of thing boils me up to the value of three."

"Yes. And if you do find him, leave enough of him for me. I want to know who he's dealing with."

"I'll try. I'll be phoning you."

The line goes dead.

I'm back at the flat sitting on the edge of my unmade bed with the smell of the sheets reminding me of Audrey. An hour ago I got on to Con McCarty to go down to Richmond and have a look at Mallory's house and I'm waiting for his call.

I get up and pour a drink and think about the time at Dulwich. After that one Gerald and Les should never have touched Jimmy again, but no, they said he's good, he knows his stuff, that was an accident, happen to anybody. Sure it was an accident, a Securicor guard lying in the gutter with a hole in his stomach, hands grabbing at the hole trying to keep himself together, and Tony Warmby frozen with the pump action still smoking and Jimmy who'd screamed at Tony to shoot now screaming at him to move, for fuck's sake move, get in the fucking car, and then putting his foot hard down and taking off half on the pavement and leaving Tony there to cop for it. Sure it had been an accident. After all, as Gerald and Les had said, we'd got away with it, hadn't we, we'd got the score, and Tony hadn't grassed and the Securicor man hadn't snuffed it. And Tony's old lady'd got his share, hadn't she? Didn't work out too bad at all. Except someone like Tony who would never grass was on fifteen to twenty and the person who'd virtually put him away was now grassing the rest of us.

The phone rings and it's Con.

"Gone away," he says. "Gone away all neat and tidy."

"You got in?"

"Yeah, I got in all right. For someone who associates with society's antisocial elements he isn't very burglarproof."

"And?"

"The works. Suits, socks, papers—you name it. Even the fridge was clear. It wasn't what you'd call a hasty decision."

"And nothing to say where to?"

"What do you think?"

"All right," I say. "I'm going over to Maurice's now. I've got Tommy Gardner looking into Jimmy's friends so you may as well go over to Jimmy's place and see what you can turn up there. Which of course will be fuck all. But it has to be done."

"And then what?"

"I don't know. Come to Maurice's and if I'm not there I'll be back at the club."

Con puts down the receiver and I put on my jacket and go out of the flat and get a taxi over to Maurice's.

I walk down the basement steps and ring the bell and the curtain at the window by the side of the door moves slightly and then a minute later the door is opened by a tall blond Adonis with a Kirk Douglas hairstyle.

"Evening, Mr. Carter," he says.

"Evening, Leo. Who's in?"

"The usual slags. The commoners. Nothing nice comes in till after midnight, not these days."

"Anybody I know?"

"Not unless you've been keeping something from me." Leo unlocks the inner door and lets me into Maurice's room.

The lighting is predominantly blush pink, the wallpaper Indian Restaurant relief. There is a small bar fitted under a Moroccan arch. There are a dozen or so small round tables and towards the back of the room there is another, larger Moroccan arch and beyond this arch there are four booth seats upholstered in red leatherette and this is where Maurice holds court, but before I go over and pay my respects I make my way to the bar. The boys are three-deep at the bar, as if they're huddling together for warmth, heads flicking this way and that like bantams on the lookout for corn, all the different shades of rinses as one under the sugary lighting, chained jewelry dulled by the atmosphere, buttocks and profiles just that little bit smoother in the dimness. And of course a straight arrival like myself causes the heads to flick and the lips to flutter even more. The whole place smells like the inside of a handbag. I manage to reach the bar without too much friction and I tell the drag barman to give me a vodka and tonic and while he's getting it for me I look in the mirror behind the bar and in the mirror is the reflection of Peter the Dutchman.

"Buy us a drink, Jack?"

The reflection has dyed blond hair and purple tinted glasses. It's wearing a coffee-coloured suit and a wide brown tie on a pink shirt. It's smiling a great ice-cream smile using all the muscles you use for that kind of smile, but I know exactly what's going on behind the purple tints. The barman waits for me to give him the nod and when eventually I do the reflection orders Campari, and sits down on the next stool but one.

"Haven't changed a bit, Jack," Peter says. And I say, "Who, Peter? You or me?" Peter the Dutchman giggles and says, "I'll never change, you know that."

No, I think, you'll never change; you'll always be the sadistic puff you always were. Peter's the kind of queer who's not content with getting his pleasure with the other boys; he has to take it out on the girls as well. Looking at him, I remember a little croupier girl he took home once. I saw her a couple of days afterwards, when she'd managed to summon up the courage to come to the club to pick up her money, because there was no way anybody marked like she was going to sit at a table and encourage the customers to part with their money. I remember her well. She'd even had to buy herself a wig because Peter had cut most of her hair off for her. But thank Christ I don't have to have much contact with him. He's a specialist but he won't be doing any business with our firm as long as I'm working for it. He's just done remission on five for going over the top with someone who got in his way, and with a bit of luck the next tickle he goes on he'll do the same, and then it'll be more than five he'll be out of the way.

"Well," I say to him, "if you ever do change, don't waste your money on sending me a telegram."

Then Maurice sweeps over and leads me across to his alcove, ordering my drink on the move, and I have to put up with Maurice's brand of chitchat.

While I'm going through this routine with Maurice there's a commotion behind us and I turn round to see that the door has just opened and let in Walter and Eddie Coleman and their wives, pissed up to their gills and all set to make their collective presence felt on the conventions of Maurice's Club.

The Colemans, so to speak, are in the same line of businesses as Gerald and Les. That is to say, they run clubs and various other legitimate and semi-legitimate businesses, but their real activity is directed towards the payrolls and the bullion and the banks and the import and export business. The only thing they don't deal in on the scale of Gerald and Les is vice, and that's because their patch is east and the Fletchers' is west, and although they make a few bob out of it, the real money is in the west, and Gerald and Les have the west wrapped up. The Colemans would never attempt to upset that applecart, and at the same time it gets up their noses that Gerald and Les have a few vice strongholds in *their* territory and there's sod all they can do about it, without starting the kind of aggro we can all do without.

"Oh, for fuck's sake," says Maurice, getting up and catching his medallion on the edge of the booth's narrow table. "All we need. The royal family."

He unhooks himself and gets to Walter and his crowd before they can start shoving their way through to the bar. He gives them his spiel about how nice it is to see them and how it's been such a long time and why don't they come and join him in the booth while Derek gets them all a drink and it's not until Walter is halfway across the floor that he sees that I'm there, watching his progress.

Walter stops in his tracks and gives me his look and then he says to his missus, "Hear, Maur, I told you them stories was right. Jack Carter's gone butch, whatever you used to say."

Maureen screeches her head off and repeats the very funny joke to Eddie's wife, who finds it even funnier than she did.

"Hello, Walter," I say. "Seeing where your boys go on their night off?"

He laughs at that but he finds it as funny as I found his remark.

The four of them struggle into the booth, Walter and Maureen with their backs against the wall, Eddie and his wife, Shirley, on the low stools opposite them.

Five seconds after they've sat down Walter says, "All right, then, where's the fucking drinks?"

"Fucking place this is," says Eddie, lighting the wrong end of his cigarette.

"Coming, coming," Maurice shouts from beyond the throng at the bar.

"That'll be the day," Maureen says and they all fall about laughing again. Maurice ponces over again and apologises for the poor service and Walter blows him a kiss and there's more laughter.

Then Walter focuses on me again and says, "So how's your governors keeping then?"

"Nice and fat, like you two," I tell him. "It's only people like me that keep slim."

"Up the bleeding workers," Maureen says, crossing her legs so you can see right up to the maker's name.

"No good flashing in here, darling," Walter says. "The dirty looks won't be the kind you're wanting."

"Don't you fucking believe it," Maureen says and swivels round on her seat and places her elbows on the table behind her and lifts her legs in the air and opens them wide. Shirley nearly pees herself and the crowd at the bar all have heart attacks.

"Here, you fucking ponces, don't you know it's rude to ignore a lady when she winks at you?"

This is too much for Shirley who slides onto her side on the booth seat.

Walter spins Maureen round in her seat and says, "All right, keep them on. We've all seen it before."

"Not bloody lately you haven't."

"I'm the only one then. I'm telling you. Pack it in."

Maureen starts swearing at him but she's interrupted by Maurice arriving with the drinks.

"That slag behind the bar," Maurice says, dishing out. "She'll have to bleeding go."

Walter slides up the seat towards me a bit and returns to the welfare of Gerald and Les.

"So they're all right, are they? Prospering?"

I shrug. "I get my wages. That's all I care about."

"Wages." Walter throws his head back and laughs. "Wages. The jobs you've been on."

"What jobs would they be, Walter?"

"Never mind. So long as you're happy."

I have a few thoughts whether to suss Walter as to whether he's got wind of Jimmy. He probably has, but there's no reason why he should give me a helpful answer. The Colemans and the Fletchers are like steak and porridge. The only reason the four of them are still walking this earth is that they're so shit scared of each other they've never had the nerve for a face-up. They leave that kind of thing to people like me; every now and again Gerald and Les, for some reason, real or imaginary, will send me round to have a look at one of Walter's boys and every now and again some of Walter's boys do the same in our patch. It keeps the four of them happy and chuffed with the publicity the papers give their apparent hardness. Not that they're soft. They wouldn't be the Fletchers and the Colemans if they were. It's just that they've built up their legends so strong that they don't want to put the reality to the test. So they try and fuck each other in every other way they can think of.

"Only one thing, though," Walter says. "I hope you never wish you hadn't turned me down."

"Hello, what's this?" says Maurice, who's adopted the role of magnanimous old queen by drawing up a stool between Maureen and Shirley and draping his flowered arms round their shoulders. "Something I haven't heard about?"

Walter gives Maurice the eyeball treatment and says, "We're talking, son," and because of the way Walter snaps up I realise he's not as drunk as he appears to be. But of course that's typical Walter. Even when he's out with the family he has to keep a part of himself cold and wide open so that no one gets ahead of him.

He turns back to me and says, "Yes, my son, I hope you never wish you'd done that."

What he's talking about is the time when Gerald and Les had set about Charlie Akester with a couple of iron bars and the pair of them had got carried away and they'd had to go to the trouble of driving out to Epping and leaving Charlie in the forest. They'd had bad luck and some ramblers had found the grave and it had been touch and go whether Finbow was going to be forced to do Gerald and Les because of the size it had been given in the papers. Walter had been certain they were going to go down and he'd got to me one night at the Stable and in front of the overcoats that walk behind him he'd put his proposition. When I turned him down he'd nearly lost his bottle but that had been his own fault for bracing me in public. He could have stood it if he'd been discreet. And ever since then he's been looking for the day when he can get his face back by seeing me nose down in a pile of shit. But the news for Walter, and he knows it, is that that day will never come, and the knowledge makes him even more screwed up than ever. But then what Walter doesn't know is that the reason I turned him down was that if Gerald and Les had got topped there would have been no need for me to seek alternative employment. Audrey and me would have carried on the Old Firm, running it on their behalf, which with Gerald and Les away for twenties would have been the same as having a firm of my own. But since they didn't, I can't move, not that I'd ever move to Walter. I can't move, work a firm on my own, because if I did Mal, Gerald and Les would make sure their law would put me away just to teach me a little lesson.

So I say to him, "There's only three things in life I regret, Walter. Not belting my old man harder when I left home, not going back and giving him another one, and the fact that he's dead so I can't give him any more."

Walter forces appreciation onto his face and pretends to forget his passing remark and says, "In that case let's have a drink with your old man. Maurice, get some more in will you? Jack's old man's buying."

Maurice begins to get up but Maureen, who's been giggling with Shirley about something, says, "No, don't you; let Yvonne de Carlo behind the bar fetch them."

Maurice looks a bit apprehensive but he can't afford to put a foot wrong in this company so he calls to the bar for the drag queen to bring the drinks over.

"What you up to, then?" Walter says to Maureen.

"Fun and games," she says. "Fun and games. All right?"

Walter shrugs and downs what's left of his drink. Eventually the queen totters from behind the bar and manages to make it over to the booth and comes to rest next to Maureen and plants the tray down on the table.

"Who's having what?" Maureen says.

The queen tut-tuts and Maurice says which drinks go to me and Walter and Eddie and the queen mutters something under her breath about ladies.

"You what?" Maureen says.

The queen bends over the table and starts passing the drinks out without answering Maureen which of course is just what Maureen's hoping for.

"I'm talking to you, not your arse," Maureen says.

There is still no answer so Maureen says, "I'll show you who the bleeding ladies are," and shoots her hand straight up the queen's skirt and she must have fastened on to whatever equipment has defied the scotch tape because the queen lets out a shattering shriek and tries to loosen Maureen's grip but all she succeeds in doing is to overbalance across the table. Shirley reaches forward and snatches off the queen's wig. The queen stops trying to undo Maureen's grip and flails out to try and get the wig back but Shirley flings it high in the air and the wig bounces off the ceiling and lands on the floor near the bar. Maureen must have flexed her fingers even more because the queen shrieks again and begins to slide off the table until she is on all fours and still Maureen doesn't let go and the queen begins to crawl in the direction of her wig, Maureen straddling her, still grasping whatever it is she's got hold of. The queen groans and squeals and tries to grab the wig but when she gets within reaching distance Maureen puts one knee in the small of the queen's back so that the queen is no longer on all fours but face down on the floor with Maureen sitting on her. Then Maureen rips the back of the queen's dress so that it's completely in two from neck to hem, leans forward and picks up the wig and stuffs what she can get of it down the back of the queen's drawers.

Then Maureen gets up and says, "Who's the bleeding lady now, then?"

All the time this has been going on Walter and Eddie and Shirley have been clapping and cheering and Maurice has been wetting himself but not daring to do anything about it. The boys at the bar have been watching all a-twitter but none of them dared to interfere because they all know who Walter and Eddie are. Maureen comes back to the table and a couple of the boys help the queen to her feet and offer hankies but the queen rejects them and rushes into the ladies' room.

"Looks like Maureen's solved your problem for you, Maurice," Eddie says.

"I only kept her on because there's a shortage," Maurice says. "Where am I going to get another from?"

"Advertise that the wig comes with the job," says Walter. Just as Walter's speaking the club door opens again and Leo the doorman comes in and walks over to our table and gives me a sealed envelope.

"Whoops," Maureen says. "Looks as though Wally was right."

Leo goes away and I ignore Maureen and open the envelope and the note inside says:

> *I am in Poland Street in my car.*
> *F.*

I put the note in my pocket and get up.

"Here," Maureen says, "he's off for a cuddle in the cloak-room."

"Yeah, he's going to kiss Leo behind the hangers," Walter says. "Get it?"

They all start falling about again but I don't bother to say anything because I'm too interested to see what's so important that Herbert Finbow can't speak to me about it in Maurice's Club.

Finbow

THE CAR IS FULL OF Finbow's cigarette smoke. Finbow's sitting behind the wheel, staring in the direction of the girls across the road who are trying to drum up custom for the near-beer palace they're out in front of. But Finbow's not seeing them. Finbow's seeing things in his mind that are making his complexion worse than the sodium shining into the car ever could. He looks like a cod on a slab. I ease into the seat beside him and close the door. Finbow carries on staring in the direction of the girls so I get my cigarettes out and he takes a fresh one from me without altering the direction of his gaze. I light his cigarette for him and then I light mine. Finbow inhales without taking the cigarette from his mouth and instead puts both hands on the steering wheel and bows his head so that the cigarette smoke wreathes upwards round his ears making his head look like a boar's that's just been served up on a plate. He stays like that for a minute or two then he raises his hand and pushes it into his inside pocket and takes out a snapshot and passes it across to me. I look down at the photograph. It's not a very good one, considering the camera that's taken it. The group of figures that's sitting round the wrought-iron terrace table is all to one side, and a little bit out of focus, not quite as sharp as the bottles of champagne and the glasses on the table in front of them, but then Audrey never was much good with a camera. Although for anyone who was interested, the faces aren't blurred enough to disguise the identity of their owners; me, and Gerald and Les, and Finbow, on the terrace of Les's house outside Camberley. Everybody's smiling although Finbow wouldn't have been if he'd known the picture was being taken.

I turn the picture face down on my lap and I don't really have to ask but I ask anyway. "What are you showing me?"

"I'm showing you the picture that's going to be on the front page of the *Daily Express* tomorrow morning."

I nod and turn the picture over and look at it again.

"Somebody owed me something and they brought it over," Finbow says. "Not that it'll do me any good. They didn't owe that much."

"Do you know how they got it?"

Finbow shakes his head.

"And we thought you were in with Swann," I tell him.

"I wish I fucking well was."

"Why didn't you get in touch with us?"

"I've been trying to find out what's going on." For the first time Finbow turns his head and looks at me. "But I can't. Nobody'll talk to me. Not one of the fuckers. They must have known this was coming off. The cunts must have known and not one of them talked to me."

I don't say anything.

"I'm finished, Jack. I'm fucking finished."

I roll down the window and let some air in.

"Did Gerald and Les send the picture in?" Finbow asks.

"You must be fucking joking."

"Then why the picture? Why take it?"

"Gerald and Les like a record of the celebrities they mix with."

"Yes."

"So what's going to happen?"

Finbow shakes his head. "It's a setup. I mean, the Commissioner already knows about the picture. It'll do him good, the incorruptible Commissioner winkling out the rotten apples, acting immediately, suspension pending an inquiry. Statements to the press giving him a chance to show everybody how straight he is. And of course I'll resign before the inquiry, just to prove he's right. No two ways about that."

While Finbow's going on about the prospects of his old age I'm thinking about the photograph and how it got to the *Daily Express*. Outside of me and Audrey the only person who knows about the Fletchers' photographic collection and where it's kept is Mallory. So, all right. It's Mallory who's organised the picture being lifted and Mallory's definitely in on Swann's deal. So what extra does he get out of shopping Finbow? Not just to make things extra uncomfortable for Gerald and Les. When Jimmy Swann talks they'll have all the discomfort they need.

I throw my cigarette out of the window and interrupt Finbow's stream of consciousness by saying, "How did you find out about Swann if nobody's talking to you?"

"What? Oh, yes. From the appearance register. They didn't bother about that. I sniffed out all the secrecy, Christ, you couldn't miss it. But by the time I found out it was too late."

"Cross knew. It was him that told us."

Finbow closes his eyes and smiles. "Sure. And by now he'll be nose-first up the arse of whoever it is that's shopping me."

Over the road a punter who's been walking up and down past the girls finally braces up and stops and the girls begin to go into their routine.

"So what next?"

"Tomorrow I get the press. Tonight I try and work out some kind of statement. The *Express* has been on already for quotes to go with the picture."

"And?"

"Unavailable for comment, aren't I? Until tomorrow. And then there'll be no way I can dodge the bastards."

"What are you going to tell them?"

"How about we're all in the same lodge?"

Con McCarty's Scimitar drifts past and continues on round the corner. There's no doubt that he's seen us. Con doesn't miss much but he'd never stick his nose into a situation unless he was told to. He'll go on to Maurice's just like we've arranged.

"Anyway," I say to Finbow, "I must be off."

Finbow looks at me. "Just like that?"

"Sure. Sitting here with you isn't going to make things better."

"But what about afterwards? After I've resigned? I've got commitments. I'm not a rich man, you know."

"You could have fooled me."

"But if anything went wrong, it was always understood that I'd be seen all right, afterwards."

"Then speak to Gerald and Les about it. Afterwards."

I flip the photograph onto Finbow's lap and get out and close the car door and begin to walk back to Maurice's. Finbow makes me want to throw up. He's made more out of Gerald and Les per year than the Chairman of Woolworth's makes out of his firm. And now he's got to stop being one of the filth and he's suffering from the shits. Christ, you'd think he'd be glad to be out of it, glad to be able to be a genuine villain for a change.

Leo opens Maurice's front door for me again and Walter and Eddie are shrugging on their camel coats by the tiny cloakroom. There is no sign of their wives.

"Can't stay away, can he?" Eddie says.

"I had to go out for a breath of fresh air," I say, looking at Walter. "Now you're going I won't have to do it again."

"Oh, Jesus," Leo says, passing a hand across his eyes.

Walter takes a couple of slow steps towards me, fastening his coat as he approaches.

"One day, Jack," he says, "you and me are due for a face-up. The only thing that worries me is that you're such a fucking chancer that something might happen to you before I had my turn. I'd be really disappointed if it did, if something happened to you first."

I smile at him.

"It might," I say. "You know, like being pumped in the back, or run over on my way to work, or blown up in my car. Something brave like that. Eh, Walter?" Walter's face loses any expression it may have had and his hands stop at the bottom button of his coat and he's trying to come to terms with himself as to whether it should be here and now, but before he can reach a decision the door to the bar opens and Maureen and Shirley come through filling the small space with their high-pitched voices. Walter decides what to do and buttons the final button and turns to Maureen and Shirley and gives them his slow hard look and they shut up.

I turn my back on Walter and walk through into the bar. The boys are still twittering about what happened to the queen. Con is sitting at a table on his own, his leather coat still buttoned and belted and his leather trilby with his gloves folded neatly on top lying on the table in front of him. Next to the hat is a pint glass half full of lager and two empty lager bottles standing next to it. I wonder where they've dug up a pint glass in a place like this.

"Want another?" I ask Con.

Con looks at his drink.

"I don't exactly *want* any more of this piss," he says. "But that's the nearest they get to beer in this dump."

I give the nod to Maurice who's taken over behind the bar and sit down at the table.

Maurice brings the drinks over and while he's putting them on the table he says, "If those bitches didn't own the license I'd bar the door to them."

"That wouldn't stop them if they wanted to come in," I tell him. "In any case, they only come in to show off because it's the only piece of property they've got round here. Take no notice of them."

"Try telling my staff that."

Maurice goes away and Con says, "Wally been having fun?"

"Forget that. What about Jimmy's place?"

"Same as Mallory's. Nothing."

I take a drink.

"Well, what did you expect?" Con says.

"Nothing."

"So what next?"

"He could be anywhere. Fucking anywhere."

"The only chance is a grass."

"Yeah. But where does the grass get his information from? The filth is closing ranks."

Con laughs. "Since when?" he says.

"Since tomorrow morning. Read the papers for once."

What I like about Con is that he doesn't ask for an explanation like anybody else would. He just takes a sip of his drink and if I don't tell him any more that's all right with him.

"Who else is in this one?" Con asks.

"I've got Tommy doing some sniffing but that's all. Who else is there?"

"You could put a price out. You'd pull a few then."

"That's up to Gerald and Les. They might not want to right now."

"So what do we do?"

"I'm going to have to have a go at Cross again. He's trying to row out now Jimmy's going to spill. But Cross always knows more than he lets on. In the meantime I thought we'd go down east and have a look at Jimmy's brother-in-law. That's the closest family that's still walking about."

While I'm talking the loo door opens and the barmaid appears, having had a crack at restoring herself to her former glory. There are a few sniggers from the boys whose moral outrage had been oiled a bit since the incident and from Maurice behind the bar there is complete ignoration. The queen makes sure that there are no members of the Coleman family hidden in the alcove and begins to make her way to the door, trying to catch Maurice's eye and extract some sympathy, but Maurice carefully inspects a glass he has just polished until the queen has reached the door.

"Rotten fuckers, the lot of you," the queen shrieks and slams the door behind her.

"Is that what Walter was playing with?" Con asks.

I down my drink and stand up. "I'll tell you on the way over."

Charlie

AT THE ELEPHANT I tell Con to stop the car and I cross the road to a telephone box and try to get Gerald and Les to tell them about Finbow but they're still out with the Americans. The Americans. I smile to myself. The junket boys. The jet-set setup. Gerald and Les in the big international league. But there'll only be one set of winners, and it's no use me trying to tell Gerald and Les who that's going to be. And at a time like this they're out entertaining the people who are going to take them. I haven't time to ring round all the places they might be at so I get back in the car and Con drives on to the place where we're going to find Charlie Abbott.

From the outside, the Premier Social and Sporting Club looks like a Temperance billiard hall. Inside it's not much different either except that if you pass Storey the manager a quid on top of the price of a bottle he'll provide you with whatever you feel like drinking and maybe even polish the glasses. The only other catering is hot bacon sandwiches and cups of tea and all packs of cards for the games are dispensed at the counter. The only lighting in the hall apart from the rectangles above the billiard tables comes from behind the counter, illuminating the chocolate bars and the cellophane of the cigarette packets beneath the dirty glass of the display cases. Where the billiard tables end, in the gloom at the far end of the hall, there are two double doors inset with small panes of frosted glass. Behind these doors is where the card games take place. There are several tables, none of them genuine card tables, just an assortment of the kind of cheap stuff you'd find in any living room, all arranged at random with no table better placed than another, but on any given night the centre table could be carrying a solo school at a shilling a call and the table near the tiled fireplace could be carrying a game of brag that would buy you a new Mercedes if you had the nerve to sit down to it. The two double doors are usually only open towards the beginning of an evening. The closing of the doors has nothing to do with a fear of the filth turning up and sorting everybody; often one of the filth would be involved in a game. It is just that some of the players in the higher games prefer to know by the rattling of the doors that someone is just about to enter so that if that someone were to be a body they could do without seeing they can prepare themselves for that kind of eventuality. And tonight, because of the lateness of the hour, the doors are closed and only slight movements of frosted shadows suggest that the cardroom is in use.

As for the rest of the place, it isn't exactly full of riveting action. Only two of the tables are occupied. On one of the tables a couple of old-timers are using the cues until the place closes up and they have to find somewhere else to keep warm. At the other table a four-hander is in progress, and although the Premier is an all-male establishment two of the players are girls who could be any age from sixteen to twenty-five. The only reason they're being allowed to grace the dusty gloom of the Premier is because one of the men they're with is a famous face, Ronnie Grafton, last year's leading goal-scorer in the league. But that was last year. Under the snooker lights his baby face looks a little puffier than in the papers when he's featuring in the latest in evening dress, his belly looks a bit looser, his hair is not its usually beautifully barbered self. Nor, as he stretches himself to try a shot he's never going to get, is his expression as open and angelic as it is when he races back to the centre line after scoring. Perhaps that's because he hasn't done so much scoring this season. Perhaps because the rumour is that he'll be on a free transfer to Millwall if he doesn't cut out everything except what he's supposed to do on the field. He makes the shot and he misses. His male opponent, a well-groomed hanger-on, tells Ronnie what bad luck it was and the two girls agree that it really was hard luck.

As Con and I approach the counter Con says, "He can't even do it with a stick now."

Storey is leaning on the counter, chin in hands, watching the game with the same kind of interest he'd watch an empty table. He doesn't look at us but when we get to the counter he says, "What do you two want?"

"A cup of tea and a waddy," I tell him.

"Nothing else?"

"What else is there?"

"Only last time you showed your faces in here I finished up with a broken cue and Michael Coughlan finished up with three broken fingers."

"I offered to pay for the tape."

"Tape didn't help the cue."

"Well, the thing was, it was one of your bent ones and Michael very kindly suggested I tried to straighten it on his fingers."

Storey calls to his wife to get us two bacon sandwiches and two cups of tea and then he says, "I thought he'd be enough for one night." He nods in Ronnie Grafton's direction, who's pouring a large Scotch into a glass balancing on the edge of the snooker table. Judging by the sweat on his forehead he doesn't exactly need another large one. "Now I get you two. Who are you looking for?"

I shake my head. "Snooker. We just felt like a game of snooker and a bacon sandwich."

Storey lifts himself off the counter and opens the flap. "In that case I'll rack them up for you. Just to make sure."

Storey strolls over to one of the tables and slides the triangle around on the baize. Con and I lean against the counter and watch Ronnie Grafton's game. It's the turn of the girl he's playing with to make her shot.

She's got a red on the edge of a pocket with the cue ball a couple of inches away from it and on the edge of the opposite pocket there is the black to follow. She is facing away from us and when she leans over the table her skirt rides up and Con and I are given a treat. Grafton sees what we're seeing and doesn't like the fact that we don't look away when he turns his gaze on us. The girl makes her shot and all she manages to do is move the red to the opposite side of the pocket.

"Jesus Christ," Grafton says. "I don't fucking believe it."

The girl straightens up and begins to apologise but Grafton cuts in on her and says, "You're bleeding useless, aren't you? Pigging useless. Nobody but you could miss a shot like that."

"I don't know," Con says to me, but loud enough for Grafton to hear. "I thought it was rather a nice angle myself."

"Yes," I say. "And she must be fond of Ronnie, too. She even wears his colours."

Grafton puts his cue down on the table and walks over to us.

"All right," he says. "Who are you two?"

"Scouts for Millwall," I tell him. "We need a new ball boy. Interested?"

Grafton smiles. "Oh yeah," he says. "A couple of those. Wherever I go, there's always a couple of those. Can't fucking stand it, can you, you being you and me being me."

"Who is he, Con?" I say.

Con shakes his head.

"You can't stand it, can you? Can't stand the money I make or the birds I pull."

"I could stand her anytime," Con says.

"Well, I'll tell you," Grafton says. "I don't like chancers looking up my girlfriend's drawers, right?"

"Then tell her to wear longer skirts or give up snooker," I say.

"And I don't like clever cunts, either," Grafton says.

"Ronnie," says Storey, beginning to drift away from the snooker table in Grafton's direction.

"And I'm going to show you how much I don't like chancers looking up my girlfriend's drawers."

"Ronnie," Storey says again.

"Shut your face."

"Ronnie, this is Jack Carter and Con McCarty and they work for Gerald and Les."

The remark manages to stop Grafton swaying for a second or two. He looks at us both, looking properly now, checking the way we look against what Storey's just said. It doesn't take him long. And now he begins to ask himself how he's going to be able to back down after styling himself so brave.

"Go back to the game, Ronnie," Storey says. "You've got some points to catch up."

There's really nothing else for him to do. He tries out his hardest look on us but he's still got to turn away and when he gets back to his table he starts on his mate by asking him what's he waiting for and why hasn't he started his shot yet. Storey goes back behind the counter and Storey's old lady arrives with the tea and the waddies.

"He ought to be grateful to you," Con says.

"I'm not doing him any favours," Storey says. "I've got a bet on Saturday's match."

I take a bite of my bacon waddy.

"Decent game in there tonight, is there?" I ask Storey.

Storey takes a packet of Weights from his cardigan pocket and sticks one in his mouth and says, "There's a couple of games. Depends what you call decent."

"Depends on who's playing. A game's only as good as the players."

"And the next question is who's playing in them," Storey says. "Jesus, Jack, you think I'm fucking barmy?"

"Listen, I've told you. Like I tell everybody. It's worth a trip down here just for the bacon waddies. Best bacon waddies in London, these are."

Storey lights his cigarette and shrugs.

"I'm past caring," he says. "I really am. If there's going to be trouble there's going to be trouble. There's sweet fuck all I can do about it."

"There'll be no trouble, Mr. Storey," Con says. "On that you have my word as a good Catholic."

I finish my sandwich and pick up my cup and saucer.

"I think I'll stroll through and have a little look," I say to Con. "You follow me through in a minute."

Carrying my cup and saucer, I walk over to the double doors and open one of them and slide through and close the door behind me.

There are two games in progress. The small one is Black Lady for a shilling a point and at the centre table it is three-card brag, five players, a pound a round. Sitting at this table there is Albert Hill, Donald Mouncey, George Longman, Bob Shearer and Charlie Abbott, who is the brother-in-law of Jimmy Swann. Hill and Mouncey supply Gerald and Les's shops with material which they make themselves. I wonder if Charlie knows that his sister is one of Hill and Mouncey's biggest stars. Probably, because if there was touchable money around Charlie would be the first to know where it lay. Hill is in his late twenties, an ex-cameraman who formed his own production company to make commercials, a perfect setup for producing the stuff that by my calculations brings them in between thirty and forty thousand a year. Mouncey is Hill's sideman, organizing the pulling and the packaging and the delivery of the goods to Gerald and Les. Mouncey's a couple of years older than Hill and they both think they're smarter than they really are. They tend towards the idea that they supply the goods, so Gerald and Les need them, instead of it being the other way round. But they don't cause any trouble and they deliver the stuff so Gerald and Les allow them their delusions, content in the knowledge that one day they'll learn the hard way about the things they should have been bright enough to realise for themselves. The other two, Bob Shearer and George Longman, are hired hands who do this and that and sometimes they're lucky enough to pick up a grand, top wack, and when they pick up anything in that region they're down here to see if they can double it, but the way they play they're lucky if they only halve it. And that leaves Charlie Abbott who greets me like he greets everybody else, as if I'm the man from the insurance company.

"Jack," he says, "Jack Carter. Christ, it's been months."

The only way to describe Charlie is to say that he looks as if he ought to have been in Jimmy James's music hall act. He's wearing a good shirt but the collar is two sizes too big and the tie which would have fetched a price from Arthur English is knotted so that the thin end straggles down to the bottom of his fly and the fat end just about reaches the bottom end of his breast pocket. The suit is new but not good; judging the way Charlie keeps shrugging his shoulders he feels like a million dollars, a phrase that must have been current when his taste in clothes was formed. His glasses shine like an expression of his pleasure on seeing me walk into the cardroom. The remaining strands of hair on the top of his head glisten with Brylcreem under the naked light bulbs.

"Hello, Charlie," I say, "Hello, Albert."

Albert is pleased that I've singled him out to be acknowledged. He's that kind of character, builds himself up on the names he thinks salute him, shoots the shit to the people who find those names impressive. Charlie is something else again. Whereas Albert basically realises he's lucky to be given the nod, Charlie really believes that people are as pleased to see him as he is to see them. He's high on the excitement of his brother-in-law's success, exhilarated by the fact he can always put the touch on his sister, so he doesn't have to fail at trying to draw a few bob ever again. The closest Charlie ever got to success in his own right was when he sat behind the counter in one of Gerald and Les's shops and drew a shilling for every punter's note he took, but even then he had a bit of bother with his accounting system and it was only because Jimmy Swann spoke up for him he avoided getting some attention from Gerald and Les. And because Jimmy's so heavy Charlie basks in his reflected light, imagining himself to be on the same level, deluding himself that he's respected the same way Jimmy's respected. Or was.

"Want to come in on this one, Jack?" Charlie says. He beams round the table at the others. "That'll be all right, won't it, lads?"

That's the kind of fucking stupid thing Charlie says. There would be no way it wouldn't be all right if I wanted to sit down. The door opens and Con comes in.

"No thanks, Charlie," I say. "Leave me out of this one."

"Good school, Jack," he says. "Good school. We're all very good players here. You'd enjoy the action." Con winces and I now know who the asthmatic was who always sat behind me at Saturday morning pictures repeating the American phrases that glided down from the screen.

I shake my head. "I've had enough excitement for one night, Charlie. You carry on."

"Been on a tickle have you?" Charlie says, looking at the others again, to see if they're admiring his familiarity, but all they do is avoid his eyes so that they can be left out of any embarrassing repercussions that might be caused by his lack of tact. I don't answer Charlie.

Instead I take a sip of my tea and Albert says, "Come on, Charlie. Let us know what you're doing."

They're playing a version of brag where you're dealt three cards, two face up, the third blind, and gamble against what your opponents might have face down, taking into consideration of course what you already see, and not knowing what you have face down yourself. Charlie has ace and three of spades showing, Bob Shearer has ten of spades and four of hearts, Albert five of diamonds and three of hearts, George Longman jack of spades and nine of spades. Mouncey has thrown in his hand so on the showing cards Charlie has the best chance with the ace, and he could have a flush, but then Albert could have a run, George could have a run or a running flush, and all of them could have nothing like Bob with his ten and his four.

But as Charlie has the psychological ace he's very happy with the present state of affairs so he says, "I'm carrying on bragging, Albert, that's what I'm doing."

He grins at me as if I'm the only one in the room who appreciates his card-playing ability and floats another pound across the table. Albert follows him and so do the other two and inside a couple of minutes the pot is twenty quid heavier. At this point, George Longman tells the table he's going to have a look and slides his blind card to the edge of the table and flicks the card with his thumb and the card snaps back face down and George is thoughtful for a while.

"All right," he says. "I'll go with you."

For the privilege of looking at his third card George now has to pay double what the blind men are paying. How long he is prepared to continue paying two to one depends on how good his hand is or how far he's going to bluff a bad one. Personally, I think he's bluffing because George never had a good hand in his life; a bent dealer would never have to worry about George because he just naturally attracts all the shit in creation. Why he bothers to sit down at all I'll never know. But he carries on throwing his money in and he's just on the point of deciding whether or not to cut his losses when his mind is made up for him by Albert having a look at his own blind card to see if it goes with the five and the three and deciding that he wants to let the others think it does by staying in.

So George says, "Fuck it, then, I'm out."

Charlie gives a knowing smile and now the betting's round to him.

"So," he says to Albert, "you're trying to tell me you've got three four five, are you Albert? You're a cocky little devil, aren't you? But I got this feeling, this little feeling, that you're trying to bluff old Charlie out of what is due to him and what is rightfully his. So, the case being that you can't see a blind man, I'm going to make you sweat a little bit, Albie, my little lad." Charlie takes his wallet out, eases out some notes and slips the wallet away again.

Then with the kind of gesture that goes with a cod sleight-of-hand trick he places a fiver on the centre of the table. Albert looks at the fiver without any change of expression and thinks about it and then selects ten singles from his stack and pushes them into the middle. Charlie grins again as if he's sussed everything out, everything's as he reckoned it would be, and Bob throws his hand away.

"There's bluffing and there's bluffing," he says, reaching for his bottle of light ale. But before he can wrap his fingers round it Con has leant forward and lifted the bottle to his lips. Bob watches Con while Con drinks but he doesn't say anything.

Con puts the bottle back on the table and says to me, "I know it's only Courage, but it tastes very sweet after Maurice's piss."

Bob still doesn't say anything but leaves the almost empty bottle on the spot where Con put it. In the meantime Charlie has donated another fiver to the kitty and now he sits back happy, confident that Albert's going to stack.

But instead of stacking Albert digs into his suiting and excavates a pile more money and says, "Here you go, then, Charlie. I'm fucking barmy, as you well know, but I'm putting in forty, so it's down to you for twenty, all right?" Charlie's glasses shimmer a bit and he has a good old think. Is Albert or is he not conning him, Charlie's thinking. He must be, he thinks, because Charlie hasn't even looked at his third card yet. Yes, that's it, Albert's trying to buy the pot, and besides, Charlie can't be seen to avoid a twenty-quid raise in front of Con and myself so he pushes in his corner and sits back waiting to be proved right. Albert keeps his face straight and pushes in another forty quid. This makes Charlie even more convinced that Albert's bluffing but being the person he is Charlie just can't bring himself to back his judgment so he drops a lot of face by picking up his third card and taking a look. It's Albert's turn to smile to himself but his expression is nothing to the one Charlie assumes when he sees what his third card is. He looks as though he's just thrown away his sticks at Lourdes with the organ playing and the sun streaming through the stained-glass windows. He's got his spade and he's made his flush. So Charlie now has to pay the same as Albert and not only does he do it with a will, he ups it by another twenty, making his contribution sixty quid in all. Con looks at me and we don't even have to shake our heads. For the second time Charlie sits back and waits for Albert to pay up and look sick. But Albert is looking far from sick when he separates one hundred notes from his pile and arranges them in the middle of the table. Now it's up to Charlie to back his flush or macaroni his strides. He's beginning to wonder whether Albert's got the four after all. He can see Albert but if Albert's bluffing Charlie's going to look fucking stupid in front of us. And if Albert's got the four he's still going to look stupid. Either way it's going to cost him another hundred. Two, if Albert doesn't see him next time. Charlie ponders for a while and then he takes his wallet out again, only this time the flourish is missing. He draws out some more fivers and manages to make them add up to a hundred and puts them in the middle although Charlie's fingers make it look as though he's trying to take the notes out. Charlie withdraws his lingering hands and now Albert's really got him. Albert gives Mouncey the nod and Mouncey opens up his wallet and adds a sheaf to Albert's pile and Albert arranges the notes into a neat oblong and places it next to Charlie's disheveled contribution.

"Two hundred," Albert says. "Two hundred to go, Charlie."

Bob Shearer tries to stop himself laughing and the sound comes out like a snort. Charlie looks as though somebody's told him he forgot to post a winning coupon.

"Two hundred?" he says. "Two hundred?"

Albert nods.

"You're not seeing me?"

Albert shakes his head.

Charlie raises his hand to wipe his lips but he's only imagining that they're wet. He stares at Albert's neat pile of notes as if it's about to jump at him.

"You can always see me, Charlie," Albert says. Charlie manages to force a grin. He's got to make the best of things now. He shakes his head.

"No," he says, still managing to maintain the smile. "No, no thanks. I'm not paying you two hundred just so you can show me the four."

"Stacking?" Albert says.

Charlie's smile disintegrates as he nods to Albert and Albert shrugs and leans across the table and rakes in the pot. Charlie lights a cigarette and tries to show us that it wasn't very important anyway.

"Jesus, Jack," he says. "I really thought the bleeder was bluffing. I really didn't think he'd got the four."

"And did he?" I say.

Charlie stares at me and when he's working out what I'm saying he turns his gaze on Albert. Albert grins at Charlie and picks up his cards and turns them over. Instead of three four five, it's a pair of threes that's staring Charlie in the face.

When Charlie gets his voice back he says, "A pair of threes? I could have beaten that. I had a hand that would have beaten that."

Albert nods in agreement. "That's right, Charlie. You certainly had the better hand."

"Shame," Bob Shearer says.

Charlie scrapes his chair back and stands up. He takes a last look at the pair of threes and walks out of the cardroom. As the door swings to behind him everybody bursts out laughing.

"What a prick," Bob says. "What a flaming prick."

"Well," says Con, "that's Charlie Abbott for you."

"Come on," I say. "Let's go and prop him up with a drink. Otherwise he might be too dry to talk."

Con follows me through the frosted-glass doors. When they've closed behind us I say, "There's one thing. Charlie sure as hell knows fuck all about Jimmy. Not a thing."

"Yes," Con says. "We're wasting our time down here."

"Not entirely," I tell him. "Charlie's ignorance might even turn out to be a help."

Charlie is at the bar sorting through the remainder of his notes so that he can pay for the use of the half-bottle of scotch Storey's just put on the counter for him. By the time Con and me get to him he's already splashed out a tumblerful and he's sucking it up, eyes closed, trying to blank out the last five minutes.

"Bad luck there, Charlie," I say. "I would have backed him having the four, if I'd been sitting down." Charlie opens his eyes and begins to feel a little better, managing to forget the money for a moment.

"Yeah, right," he says. "But that's cards, isn't it, Jack, eh? That's what it's all about. Sometimes you're up, sometimes you're down, isn't it?"

"That's right, Charlie."

Then Charlie remembers his manners.

"Cliff," he says to Storey, "get two more glasses, will you? Jack, you'll have a drink, won't you? And Con?"

"May as well," Con says.

"Charlie," I say, "can I have a quiet word?"

Charlie's just picking up the new glasses and when I tell him I want to talk to him, all of a sudden he's on the verge of doing the macaroni. Now he knows that I've come all the way down here to see him, and reasons why start flashing through his mind while he stands there like a waxwork with the glasses in his hand. I pick up the scotch and pour some in the glasses then I take the glasses from him and pass one of them to Con.

"Don't worry, Charlie," I tell him. "It's only a word. Nothing for you to worry about."

"What do you want, Jack?" Charlie says.

"Let's take our drinks over to the corner and I'll tell you."

We move away from the counter and over to the far side of the hall, where there is a long bench seat on a platform raised six inches off the floor and flush to the wall. Charlie sits down on the bench and Con and myself sit down on either side of him. The two games which were in progress earlier are still going on but they're right down the other end of the hall. All the other table lights are switched off and where we are the only illumination is the counter's reflection in Charlie's glasses.

"Been in touch with your sister lately?" I ask Charlie.

"Jean?" he says, looking from me to Con and back again. "I haven't seen Jean in a fortnight. Maybe longer. Why, has she—"

I cut him off short. "She hasn't been in touch with you?" I say. "Tried to phone you or anything?"

"No, not that I know of. I mean, I move about a bit, you know, she might have tried to, but—"

"But you might be wanting to get in touch with her after tonight, eh, Charlie?"

It takes Charlie a minute or so to tumble.

"Oh, see what you mean," he says, trying to accept the baldness of my statement as if it's some kind of affectionate joke. "Well, you know, Jean's always been very good to her old brother, never sees me short, like. You know, I get things wholesale for her and she sees me all right, understand. I mean, after tonight I'll perhaps be getting in touch because she owes me for one or two bits and pieces.

Didn't intend dropping so much in the game, know what I mean?"

"So what'll you do? Go round the flat and see or meet her or what?"

"Well, it's not always too convenient to go straight round, just like that. I mean, Jimmy works hard and he likes a bit of peace and quiet during the day, and evenings they're out mostly . . . "

"You'd just phone her up, then? Find out where she's going to be."

"Something like that, yes."

"Pity," I tell him. "Because, like, the next time you phone I shouldn't hang on too long waiting for a reply."

Charlie looks at me, not daring to ask.

"Nothing like that," I tell him. "Just that her Jimmy's been pulled by Old Bill. And since they pulled him, Jean and the kids have dropped out as well. We just had a sort of vague idea you might be able to put us in the picture. Let us know where Jean is so we can find out what's going on. You see, Charlie, we really need to find out what's going on."

Charlie stares at me as if he hasn't believed a word I've said to him.

"Jimmy?" he says. "They've picked up Jimmy? But they wouldn't. He's like you. They wouldn't pick up Jimmy."

"They have done. And it'll be me and Con and Gerald and Les filing in one after the other if we don't find Jimmy."

"But Jimmy'd never grass. Jesus, everybody knows he'd never do that."

I don't answer him.

"Jack? He wouldn't, would he?"

"He probably already has done."

Charlie tries to find his cigarettes, so to save time I give him one of mine and light it for him. He takes a few drags and then manages to put words to what he's been thinking about.

"If you find Jimmy, what'll happen?"

"Depends on Jimmy. If our information's wrong, we'll give him all the help we can, the way Gerald and Les help everybody they do business with. So let's hope our information's wrong, eh, Charlie?"

Charlie takes a pull at his whisky.

"I couldn't do it even if I knew how, Jack," he says. "Not to my own brother-in-law. Not to Jean's husband."

"Jimmy hates your fucking guts, Charlie. He's the reason Jean doesn't drop you as much as she used to. That's why you never go round their place and get to see your nephew and your niece. So don't shoot the shit. If Jimmy can put you in this one he will."

"Jean'd never let him. She'd never let him do that to me."

"Jean does as she's bleeding well told. Especially to keep Jimmy off a twenty-five stretch."

"Jack, listen. If they're not at home, how will I know where they are? They could be bleeding anywhere."

"Tell me something I don't know, Charlie."

Charlie shakes his head. "Leave me out, Jack. You know I can't help."

"Your old mother might, though. I mean it's just possible your sister might get in touch with her dear old mum so's she won't have to do any unnecessary worrying."

"Christ, you wouldn't involve her, would you?" Charlie says.

I don't answer his question but instead I say to him, "Look, Charlie, I want to stop pissing about. I really do. So I'm going to put alternatives to you as clearly as I possibly can, and I want you to listen to them as hard as you possibly can, because I'm not going to tell you again. One of the alternatives will just happen, right? Now. You can help us and in helping us you can do yourself a bit of good, because I can speak for Gerald and Les in saying that if Jimmy comes a cropper then Jean and the kids will be looked after, and if you're Jack the Lad and help us they'll look after you too. Either way you don't lose. Where you do lose, Charlie, and where the rest of your family lose, is if we get no cooperation. Whether we find Jimmy or not is beside the point. Gerald and Les will want Jimmy to know how they feel, and they won't care who they use to show him. So all that I'm telling you is for your own good. You see that, Charlie, don't you?"

In the following silence Con, who has been watching Grafton's game, says, "That bastard's still giving that little girl the shitty end of the stick."

"Yeah, well forget it," I tell him. "We're here on business, not pleasure."

Charlie treads his cigarette into the floorboards.

"All right," he says. "I'll help you. I'll do what I can."

"That's the idea, Charlie."

Charlie stands up. "In fact I'll drop over there tonight. You never know, the old girl might have heard from Jean already."

He begins to move away from us.

"Charlie," I say.

Charlie stops in his tracks and looks at me. He relaxes and says, "I suppose I knew you'd want me to stick with you. I just . . . "

His voice trails off and he slumps into his suit even more.

"That's right, Charlie," I say, and put my glass down on the bench and as I turn away from Charlie he throws himself into a sprint and hares round the end of the nearest snooker table and starts to make for the double doors of the cardroom. Beyond the cardroom there is a small passage with two doors at the far end. If you go through one door you're in a karsi, and if you go through the other door you're in a back yard with a six-foot slatted fence that drops you down into Villiers Street.

"Oh, Jesus," I say. "The silly fucker."

Con is already close behind Charlie by the time I get up off the bench seat. Charlie makes the double doors and smashes them to behind him. There are angry cries from behind the frosted glass. Con yanks the doors open again and disappears from sight. By the time it's my turn to open the doors the card players have got down on their hands and knees and are trying to pick up as many notes as they can from the floor in the hope that they can argue from strength when the divvying starts. The card table is on its side in the fireplace, I imagine more as a result of Con's progress through the cardroom than Charlie's. I walk down the passage and find Con in the back yard, levered up on the fence and looking down into Villiers Street.

"No signs of the bleeder," he says, lowering himself down. "But the yard door was swinging to and fro so he must be able to move a sight faster than you'd think." Con grins at me and winks and I nod at him.

"Well, that's it, then," I say. "The crafty little bleeder's fucked us."

"Looks like," says Con. "Could be anywhere by now."

We walk back into the passage, closing the yard door behind us. We walk as far as the door that leads back into the cardroom and Con reaches forward and closes it with a rattle and we both stand there in the dark, not making a sound. After a minute or two there is the sound of the karsi bolt being drawn back and then there is more silence. Then the karsi door creaks and Charlie begins to make his exit. I can just make out his shape as he creeps over to the yard door.

I let him get as far as opening it a crack and then very quietly, I say, "Boo."

"Jesus Christ," Charlie says. "Oh, Jesus Christ," and as he says it he falls to the floor as if he's been pushed over.

Con opens the cardroom to let some light on the scene. Charlie is lying there with his arms covering his head as though he's waiting for a kicking. I walk down the passage towards him. Charlie screams but all I do is lift him up and lean him against the wall and straighten his glasses for him.

"Come on, Charlie," I say. "It's time we were going home to bed."

I put my arm round Charlie's shoulder and help him back down the passage. We negotiate our way through the cardroom and back into the billiard hall. Storey has come round to our side of the counter and is standing in the aisle made by the counter and the nearest billiard table, blocking our way to the proper exit.

He stands there nodding his head and then he says, "There was no way I could have been wrong, was there? I mean, I was right, wasn't I? The minute you came in I knew it."

"Well, you won your bet," I say, and with my free hand I loosen a couple of fivers from the roll in my inside pocket and pass them to Con, who sticks them between the salt and pepper on the counter. Storey shrugs and shakes his head and begins to walk back to his flap and we start to move towards the door again.

Then Grafton's voice breaks the silence.

"Are you having trouble, mate?" he asks Charlie.

The three of us stop and turn and there he is, standing behind us with his billiard cue gripped in both hands. I can tell he's made up for backing down by pouring even more lotion down him and if Storey offers Grafton his advice again, this time it won't make any difference.

"I said were you having some trouble?" Grafton asks. Charlie shakes his head but he can't manage to get his mouth to operate properly.

"No," I say to Grafton, "he's not having any trouble. Are you?"

Grafton lurches a little closer. "You going to give me some?"

"That depends on you," I tell him.

"Let him go," Grafton says.

I smile at him. "No," I say.

"I'm telling you," Grafton says. "Let him go."

I don't say anything and so with that Grafton tightens his grip on the cue and prepares to swing it where he thinks the side of my head is going to be. But he's so clumsy with booze that I have time to push Charlie at the billiard table and step inside the cue's arc and take hold of it just above the spot where Grafton has his grip. I pull hard and brace myself and Grafton's nose connects with my advancing forehead and just to finish it off I grab hold of his shirt as he begins to slide down my body and I give him a little tap on his shin with the point of my shoe. Grafton hits the floor and begins to hunch himself into the classic footballer's foetal position. I notice that Grafton's mate who was expressing all the concern earlier isn't exactly rushing over with a magic sponge.

Storey has his head in his hands and is staring vacantly at the top of his counter. I take another fiver off my roll and add it to the others between the salt and pepper. Then Con and Charlie and myself have another go at getting to the exit.

This time we make it and as we pass into the fresh night air Con shakes his head and says, "It's a disgrace to the game, those over-the-top tackles."

"Shouldn't ever be allowed," I say. "Could break a fellow's leg that way. Ruin his career, just like that."

Hume

ON THE WAY BACK west I try and get Gerald and Les again but they're still unavailable. Con drives very carefully so as not to give any wandering law a reason for pulling us in to the curb. Charlie sits in the back without saying a word, but he's not sitting quietly because he's found a packet of crisps in one of his pockets and he's tucking in as if he hasn't a care in the world. I'm not looking forward to having Charlie in my pocket indefinitely but when it's only this kind of long shot that's going to pay off I've got no choice but to wear him. He crunches away in the back completely unaware that there may be more than one way of getting his sister out of the woodwork.

"I want you to go to my place first," I tell Con. "Charlie'll be staying with me tonight so you take him up there and stay with him while I walk round and try to get hold of Gerald and Les. If Tommy phones take the message."

"Right," says Con.

The traffic's turning out now, most of it suburb-bound after the passengers have had a night out in London's wonderful West End. The wind has got up again and is sweeping the broad wasteland of the Elephant with sheets of drizzle.

We arrive outside my flat and I give Con the extra keys and Con helps Charlie out of the Scimitar and into my place and I slide over into the driver's seat and take the car round to the club. When I get inside I collar Alex the doorman.

"Have Gerald or Les phoned in?" I ask him.

"Not as yet, Mr. Carter," he says.

"Jesus," I say. "And they gave you no idea of where they'd be?"

"Well, they went out with the Americans so it could be the Antibes or then again it could be Arabella's Stable."

Yes, I think to myself, and knowing Gerald and Les it could be Terri Palin's house in Camden Town or some other amusement arcade. The Americans like a bit of English, especially if it is trained to act like the real upper crust. And isn't it just fucking typical of Gerald and Les on a busy night like tonight to go out without leaving their tonking address?

"Mrs. Fletcher might know," Alex says. "She's still upstairs. She's been interviewing a couple of performers."

It often happens this time of night. Girls in this particular line of work never see daylight before midday and their free time starts at 1 AM if they're lucky.

"She still busy?"

"One of the acts is still up there."

"Get her on the extension for me. I'll talk to her at the bar."

Alex walks away to his duty and I make my way through into the bar. Billy has the mixture waiting for me and presents it to me like he's auditioning in front of Nureyev. Then for the second time that night I get the tones of Peter the Dutchman's voice like treacle in my earhole.

"I'll buy my own this time," he says. "The other way's too much like hard work."

"And you'll know all about the other way," I tell him.

He slides onto the next stool but one, knowing better than to push his luck by getting on the closer one.

"Who let you in, anyway?" I ask him.

"Don't be like that, Jack," he says.

Billy the barman discreetly places himself closer to me than he does to Peter and waits. Peter asks for a Campari and soda and the barman still waits until I give him a weary nod and he goes off to do his stuff.

"Nice high-class staff you've got in here these days," Peter says, watching Billy reach up for the Campari bottle.

"Like the clientele," I say.

"Oh, that's right," Peter says, "you were asking how I got in. Well, I got in by Gerald and Les's invitation. I was on my way when you saw me in Maurice's. Dutch Courage, if you'll pardon the pun. I thought Gerald and Les would have put you in it, and I would have mentioned it only I didn't think Maurice's was the time or the place. Not for that, anyway."

The barman's extension rings and he lifts the receiver. I look at Peter.

"Put me in what?"

"Put you in why Gerald and Les are talking to me. The little tickle I've brought them. The little outing." Billy brings the telephone over to my part of the bar.

"Mrs. Fletcher," he says.

I motion for him to put the phone down.

"You've brought a job to Gerald and Les?" I say to Peter.

"That's right," he says.

"And they're buying it in?"

"Even righter."

I can hear Audrey speaking on the other end of the line. I don't want Peter's pleasure to be greater than it already is so I fake a faint grin and shake my head and pick up the receiver.

"Jack?" Audrey says.

"Yes."

"What's going on?" she says. "You didn't answer."

From the way she's talking she sounds as though she's stolen more than one or two away during the course of the evening.

I look at Peter and I say, "I can't talk right at the moment. Shall I come up?"

Audrey giggles. "You can come up anytime," she says. "All the way up."

I hope the loudness of Audrey's oiled-up voice isn't carrying as far as Peter.

"I'll come up, then."

"I don't know whether I ought to let you," she says. "I might not be able to stand the competition. I might be doing a very silly thing in letting you come up right this moment." I put the phone down before she rabbits on any longer.

"Excuse me," I say to Peter.

"Anytime," Peter says.

"Let him know where the ladies' is," I say to Billy and walk out of the bar over to the lift and I press the button and get in. This time when I get out of the lift there is a little squit called Harris sitting on the landing chair. This is something else that's typical of Gerald and Les; when they're holding court only the heaviest will do but when there's only Audrey there they put out something that wouldn't stop Tom and Jerry.

I press the button and go through the doors and once again I'm in the penthouse. Only this time instead of having the Fletcher brothers' lovely faces to gaze at there is Audrey and there is this little cracker of a West Indian sitting on the leather settee where Gerald usually sits. Audrey's standing by the stereo controls swaying a bit, a full glass in her hand.

The door slides to behind me.

"And now," says Audrey, "the Jacaranda Club proudly presents Soho's latest sensation, Claudia."

Audrey presses a button and a Shirley Bassey number starts to belt out from all four corners of the room. Claudia Cornell Wilde stands up and although she is just wearing her street clothes she begins to give an impression of what she's presumably going to be doing downstairs from next week on. Audrey does her own impression of what the spade chick's doing and wafts across the room towards me. But it isn't the time or the place for indulging in what I'd like to indulge in so I start to make for the stereo. But to get there I have to negotiate the sunken bit and I coincide with Audrey halfway across. She staggers into me and the only way to avoid collapsing on the floor is to collapse onto one of the settees. Some of Audrey's drink spills onto the front of my shirt.

She slides one of her legs on top of mine and pushes her mouth against my ear and says, "Those two bastards are out playing games at Palin's tonight so why shouldn't we play our own games here?"

"Audrey . . . "

"What's the matter? Shy are you? She'd be game, no trouble. She's high as a kite."

"Audrey . . . "

"I'd bleeding murder anybody you screwed on your own," she says. "But this'd be different." She giggles. "Besides, I'd like to see how you'd handle a bit of black. Or vice versa."

Her hand begins to slip down the front of my shirt but before she goes any farther I jerk myself up out of the leather and go over to the stereo and switch it off. The spade stops as if she's been unplugged and Audrey stares up at me from the settee.

"Business, Audrey," I say. "Or have you forgotten all about it? About the business that was discussed this afternoon?"

Audrey doesn't say anything. She knows how important the present matter is but at the same time she never likes to admit she's in the wrong or she's acted stupid.

"I've got some news that's got to be passed on," I tell her. "All right?"

Audrey straightens herself up a bit and without looking at the spade or at me she says, "All right, all right. Come back next Monday at one and we'll work out a schedule."

The spade bird doesn't move so Audrey gets up and drapes the spade bird's coat round her shoulders and helps her towards the door.

"Forget it," Audrey says. "I'll phone you when you can hear."

The door slides open and the spade bird floats out. Audrey walks over to the cocktail cabinet and pours herself another drink then makes a production out of staring through the plate glass.

"It's a pity you're Gerald's wife," I tell her.

She doesn't answer.

"Because that means I can't give you a belting without him seeing the marks."

Audrey walks back to the settee and sits down.

"You must be fucking barmy carrying on in front of that spade," I say. "Supposing she shopped you to Gerald? What do you think would happen to you then?"

"She was high. She didn't know what was happening."

"You hope. You fucking hope."

Audrey lights a cigarette and says, "Anyway, what about the business? What's the business you're so bleeding keen to talk about?"

"Where's Gerald and Les?"

"They said they were going to Arabella's first. Whether they did or not I don't know. All I do know is it's for certain they won't be there now and they won't be back before breakfast, not if they go to Palin's."

Jesus Christ, I think to myself. I walk over to the cocktail cabinet and pour myself a drink.

"Why, what's happening?"

"I don't know. Everything's going up the spout. I saw Finbow earlier and he's been shopped."

"Shopped?"

"That picture you took of us all's going to be all over tomorrow's *Express.*"

"Jesus."

"So. I think it's something Gerald and Les ought to know about, don't you?"

"But who'd want to do Finbow?"

I down my drink. "If he finds out, he'll let us know. But as Mallory's the only other person who knows about that picture outside of us four, then Mallory's got to have something to do with it, hasn't he? And Mallory being Jimmy's lawyer and Gerald and Les's lawyer makes that fact all the more interesting, doesn't it?"

I walk over to the door.

"I'm going out to try and get hold of those two characters. Not only do I have to find Jimmy Swann, I have to find Gerald and Les as well. If they get back here before I do don't tell them about Finbow. I don't want them going off half cocked and fucking things up even more."

Arabella's Stable is in Bayswater. At that time of night it only takes me five minutes to drive Con's car over there. I park it just off the Bayswater Road. The night is drying out again and scraps of cloud race across the face of a cold-glowing moon. The city's night sounds buzz away and beyond the Bayswater rooftops. The clear wind makes me feel fresher than I've felt all evening. But Arabella's will soon take care of that for me.

The usual would-be heavies are on the door. They stand there in their D.J.s with their hands behind their backs the way they think the real ones do it. Their hair is washed and blown and their sharp chins are smooth and shiny with aftershave and the hardest time any of them ever had is fighting a cold. All they ever have to do at Arabella's is take drinks away from drunks and put the drunks in taxis. But they think they're shit hot and when I show up on the steps they give me the sneer to show me how big-time they are. I smile sweetly back at them and go through into the foyer.

Leaning over the reception desk are a couple of the kind of characters I really like to do business with. Upper-crust tearaways making their gambling money by adding a Rt. Hon. or a Lord to Arabella's wages list. The hard work they do is to walk about the place asking the clients if everything's all right and at the same time making the clients feel they should be asking the tearaways instead. And as I expect when I walk over to them to inquire after my employers I get the silent treatment. I stand there for a minute or two while they study whatever it is that's fascinating them on the desk's surface and then I lean forward and put my face as close as I can to theirs without being poisoned by the hair-spray fumes and I say, "Shop."

One of them manages to raise his head an inch or so and gazes into my eyes without saying anything.

"I'm from the Prudential," I say. "I've brought you your divvy."

The tearaway continues to gaze at me.

"What is it you want?" he says at last.

"I want to speak to Minton."

The tearaway's eyes flicker just to let me know that he's weighed me up and he says, "I can assure you Mr. Minton won't want to speak to you."

"So be it," I say, and I take hold of the tearaway by his hair and drag him across the top of the desk. The tearaway screams and the tasteful ornaments smash onto the floor and I keep pulling until the tearaway is on my side of the desk. Then still holding him by the hair I walk him over to the wall and slap him two or three times in the face. "Now, then," I tell him, "I'm going to talk to Minton. I suggest you clear out your desk and pick up any ballpoint pens that might be yours and make it easy on yourself by not being here when Minton comes out to talk to you. Right?"

I let go of his hair and he slides down the wall and makes no attempt to move away from the baseboard. I walk away from him and over to the curtains that cover the entrance to the main part of Arabella's and as I part the curtains I look back and notice that the bouncers have melted from the steps.

Beyond the curtain is a small corridor and at the end of this corridor there is a flight of steps curving down to the Stable Room. The corridor is painted a very deep dark green and the pictures on the walls have been specially painted to suit the decor. It's all very tasteful and restrained which is quite ironic considering that the behaviour of the clientele is usually the exact opposite to the decor. As I descend the steps the wave of sound begins to wash over me and then I make the last turn and there before me is the Stable Room. In the first half of the room there are about twenty tables ranged round the walls and the only light comes from the small deep-red lamps on the tables. The light is so dim that you can hardly see from table to table, let alone across the room. There is about an acre of empty carpet which matches the colour of the lampshades. Beyond this room is another corridor with half a dozen curtained booths ranging on either side. The corridor leads through to the discotheque which is even darker than the rest of the place. Perhaps if the lighting was any better some well-known public figures who use the place wouldn't be down there so often.

As I'm crossing the endless carpet a figure detaches itself from one of the tables and swishes up to me.

"Mr. Carter," says the figure.

"Hello, Minton," I say. "Gerald and Les still here?"

"As far as I know, yes. I've been upstairs for half an hour. Their party's in the last booth on the left."

"Thanks."

"Nice to see you, anyway. It's been quite some time."

"Yes. Since I was last down here you've taken on some staff that doesn't know who I am."

Minton goes rigid.

"Oh no," he says. "Oh no," and turns and scuttles away to see what's happened beyond the curtains. I carry on to see if Gerald and Les are still in the third booth on the left-hand side of the corridor. I draw back the heavy velvet curtain. Gerald and Les aren't there. Instead I'm looking into the face of a man called Hume.

On the narrow table in front of Hume is a bottle of champagne on ice and sitting next to him is a girl I've never met before but she's just like the thousand others that do walk-ons in TV programs and the occasional commercial without being trained to do either. What they're really trained to do is hang out where the bread is and where the names are and when they're around it they believe that proximity breeds class. It's not really that they want the money. It's rather like the syndrome of the bird who's always pulling married men—they just want to prove they can do it. And Hume, even if he is only a Detective Inspector, has plenty of bread and he's certainly a name.

"They left ten minutes ago," says Hume. "If it's Gerald and Les you're looking for."

"Not surprising," I say.

Hume smiles and indicates the champagne.

"They insisted," he says. "They made me feel I'd really upset them if I didn't accept a drink."

The girl grins and thinks she looks knowing but all it proves is she's watched a lot of people in the same line of business.

"That's why they stayed and finished the bottle with you, is it?"

"The Americans were ready to go. Even Gerald and Les move when the Americans move." He pours some of the champagne into a spare glass. "So have a fringe benefit. I know you earn your perks."

"Don't we all?" I say as I sit down.

Hume pushes the glass towards me and I pick it up and take a sip.

"You see?" he says to his girlfriend. "Even the heavies are used to champagne these days."

"But do they appreciate it?" says the girl.

I take another sip.

"The good stuff, yes," I say, pushing the glass away.

"I don't think you've met," Hume says. "Lesley, this is Mr. Jack Carter."

"Pleased to meet you, dearie," she says, doing what she thinks is a knockout impersonation of a tart.

"I already know somebody called Lesley," I say. "Only he's going thin on top."

"Which can hardly be said for the present company," Hume says, slipping his hand in the front of Lesley's dress and easing out one of her titties and giving it a squeeze. The girl looks at me all the time, a clear cool gaze to impress on me how together she is about everything.

"Lesley's in television," Hume says. "Ever get time to watch much television, Jack?"

"Not really," I say. "Only *Thunderbirds*. You're not in *Thunderbirds*, are you?"

This time the cool slips off. "Cunt," she says.

I smile at her. Then I say to Hume, "This your night off, then? Caught your quota of thieves and robbers for today?"

"That's right, Jack," he says, still giving the thumb to Lesley's nipple. "Just hanging round here to see if I can boost the numbers."

Of all the coppers on Old Bill's wages sheet I hate, Hume's the worst. It's not just the image, the way he styles himself with his Cecil Gee suits and his Italian barbering, his TV policeman's pose. All that would be painful enough without taking his record into account. In terms of arrests and convictions he's London's most successful copper. Always in the papers, always on the box, striking dread into the hearts of villains, as the media puts it. Which is quite right, because of the way he does his work. The way he works is this: a firm pulls a job and he's got a good idea of which firm's pulled it. But he's got nothing to take to court because everybody's alibi's up and after two or three fiascos of trying to get impossible convictions he'd lose any credibility he ever had. So what he does is pull in some operator who wasn't even on the job, but because of his past record he could have been. The surprise element precludes the operator setting up an alibi, even though being innocent he doesn't feel he needs one. Then Hume, in a very honest way, puts all his cards on the table. He tells the operator that he knows he had nothing to do with the job, but that is beside the point; he is going to be charged anyway. So what it boils down to is that in return for Hume saying in court that the operator was not carrying a shooter, which will make all the difference to his sentence, the operator gives Hume a few names that will break the alibis of the people who were really involved. Hume's very careful only to drop on people who'll wear shopping their mates. He'd never touch anybody at my level, with my kind of involvement. He chooses the chancers, the ones who are more frightened by the thought of an extra three years than by a visit from friends of the people they've turned in. Hume's made a great name for himself in the papers and he's always being talked about as London's Number One thief-taker, the iron man and all that crap. Luckily for both him and us his pitch is different; his reputation wouldn't wear so well on our patch or even on the Colemans'. And what really boils up in my chest is Gerald and Les wheeling the champagne out for him, whatever the reasons, making him even more convinced of his big reputation. I only hope to Christ they weren't oiling him with the champagne to try and get something on Jimmy Swann. If it's straight law that's pulled Jimmy then Hume would be the last person to be in the picture. Any questions Gerald and Les put to Hume could only do Hume some good, like Hume finding out who's in charge and playing his own game to his own advantage, complicating things for us.

I lean over to the corner and pull the silk rope and wait for the service. Hume pours himself some more champagne and the girl tucks her titty back in her dress.

"Gerald and Les appeared to be in very good spirits," Hume says. "Business picking up? Christmas rush and that sort of thing?"

"I wouldn't know," I say. "I only work for them."

Hume takes a sip of his champagne and instead of taking the glass from his lips he goes rigid and his face becomes chalky and drops of sweat begin to squeeze out of his forehead. I shift a little bit to one side so that I don't get caught if the signs are what I think they are. The girl lights a cigarette, unaware that Hume's about to honk his lot.

Then the curtain is drawn back and the service appears and I say, "I'd like a large vodka and tomato juice and Mr. Hume would like a small tin bowl."

The service gets well out of it and Hume sets his face and tightens up his muscles and manages to hold it down. When he's settled himself down he takes the cigarette from the girl's mouth and grinds it out in the ashtray.

"What was it you said on the box the other night?" I ask him. "Villains made you feel sick?" Hume leans across the table and frames his mouth to say something and then decides to say something else.

"One day you'll shoot your bolt where I am," he says. "That day I'll be the happiest man in England. You and the Fletchers are like all the rest; you've only got so much luck."

"So long as we don't have you making our luck, we'll survive. We'll see you out, anyway."

The girl puts her cigarettes in her bag and stands up.

"Where do you think you're going?" Hume says, looking up at her.

"Nobody treats me like that," she says.

"Oh don't be so fucking stupid," Hume says, pouring the dregs of his champagne into the bucket. The girl stands there for a minute.

"Are you going to let me out?" she says.

Hume ignores her. The service returns and slides my vodka and tomato juice across the table and nips off sharpish.

"Move," the girl says.

Hume twists round on the seat and takes hold of her dress where it supports her titties and yanks her down onto the seat.

"Listen, you bitch," he says, still gripping the front of her dress, "you cock-sucking whore. Just fucking shut it or I'll shut it for you. You're here on my ticket."

The girl spits at him and tries to scratch the side of Hume's face but Hume grabs hold of her wrist and fetches her a hard one across her mouth then pulls downwards and rips the front of her dress down to the waist, causing her titties to fall out all over the place. The girl throws herself face down on the table and bursts into tears but Hume doesn't leave it. Instead he takes hold of the remains of the dress at the back and rips that off her too so she is completely naked from the waist up.

"Now then," Hume says. "Now then. Try leaving like that."

The girl stays where she is, face down on the table, sobbing.

Hume leans back in his seat and relaxes, looking like a runner after winning a sprint, chest heaving, nostrils dilated, glassy-eyed.

"Get your kicks that way, too, do you?" I say. "As well as at the verbaling sessions?"

Hume is still looking as though there's nothing between him and the wallpaper behind me.

"I used to know a bloke like that," I said. "A boxer he was. Big name. Got to be a personality on TV, just like you. Great sense of fun he had. Always laughing and joking. But offstage he used to get his thrills sorting out the weaker sex. Only one time he went too far and so as to keep out of it he cut her up and left her in various deposit boxes around London. Only one of your mob got a bit smart and put it on him. But seeing as the charmer was who he was and his club was favourite with your lot, rather than splash it all over the papers he was given the tip-off that your lads would be collecting him around eight o'clock the next morning. So instead of waiting for that he takes his shotgun out to the shed in his garden and splashes himself over the plant pots instead. Which is exactly what your mob expected would happen."

As I'm speaking Hume has gradually come back from wherever he's been.

"Yeah," I tell him. "I remember that little sequence particularly well. Used to know a little bird who fell into his scene once. Said he used to like cutting up her knickers with scissors while she was still wearing them.

According to her he couldn't make a proper job of doing what comes naturally, either."

By now Hume's fully aware of what I'm saying. A smile begins to spread over his face.

"Noble," he says. "Noble Jack. Defender of the weak. Only why don't you back your mouth?" He touches his chin with his forefingers. "Why don't you put your opinions there?"

"No," I tell him. "You've just got to keep on sweating, for me. Eat your fucking heart out, Hume."

I finish my drink and stand up.

"Are you coming, darling?" I say to the bird.

The bird lifts her face from the tabletop and stares up at me.

"It's all right," I tell her. "He's come once already tonight. He won't want you for anything else."

I take my overcoat off and pass it over to her. She doesn't touch it but instead she looks at Hume.

Hume shrugs and says, "Yes, piss off with Jack. Go home with the rest of the rubbish. Only better make sure you're not around him when I pick him one morning at eight o'clock. Because then we'd really have some fun."

The girl stands up and wraps my coat round her and climbs over Hume. I part the curtains and go into the corridor and walk along to the Stable Room and cross the carpet.

Lesley

By the time I get to the foyer the girl has almost caught me up but before she can get to me Minton materialises and takes my arm and assists my passage across to the exit.

"I'm very grateful," he says. "I really am. I should never delegate when I hire, it's always a mistake. Anyway, those two won't be making the same mistakes in here. I hope you'll accept my apologies."

The girl gets to where we are and Minton has another blue fit when he sees the state of her and uses it as an excuse to melt away again.

"Were you going without this?" she says, touching the coat that's wrapped round her.

"You must be joking," I say.

"What do you want me to do, then? Take it off here?"

"I've already seen the sights, thanks."

"Then you won't mind waiting while I get my own from the cloakroom will you?"

"No, I won't mind waiting, not for that gear. I waited long enough to get it." She gives me her fiercest look, stoked up not only by the fact that she didn't like me in the first place but also because I've been a witness to the treatment Hume's just given her. There's only one way a girl like that

73

can get her face back and I wonder if she's going to be bothered enough to try.

After she's given the look everything she can she turns away from me and makes for the ladies room. While she's off reorganizing the coat situation I go over to the now deserted reception desk and dial the number of Terri Palin's establishment. The phone rings for a long time and then the receiver is lifted and this very snotty, very businesslike female voice twangs the wires and says, "Yes?"

"Listen, I'm Jack Carter, and I know who you are as well. So don't give me the wrong-number crap. I want to speak to Terri straight away, all right?"

"I'm sorry," says the voice at the other end. "I think you must be mistaken. This is—"

"Oh for fuck's sake. Tonight I can do without it. If you don't recognise my voice just get Terri, will you, and she'll set you straight. Tell her if she doesn't come to the phone I'll be round in five minutes flat kicking in windows."

I hear the receiver rattle as the phone is laid to rest at the other end and while I'm waiting I search my pockets for a cigarette only to find I'm completely out. The foyer is empty so there's nobody I can burn off and I start to get that stupid uncontrollable need for something I can't have. And the longer I wait the more I channel the anger caused by my desire at Gerald and Les. What a pair of fucking ponces. What fucking eggs. Out tonking in the candy-floss fantasy world of Terri Palin's Disneyland. Hosting the Yanks to scenes from an English kindergarten while there's twenty-five years apiece waiting to be shared out to the stupid bastards. They're so high on their own reputations they don't really believe it's going to happen to them. And the more I think about it the more I get cross with myself for chasing about for them. If it wasn't for the fact that Jimmy Swann could score me for at least fifteen I'd just walk away from the stupid sods and leave them to sort it themselves.

I start going through my pockets for the third time when Terri Palin's voice comes over the line.

"Yes?" she says.

"Terri," I say. "It's Jack."

There is a short silence and then there is a sigh that for once isn't a piece of Terri's stock in trade.

"Jesus," she says. "I had this feeling, you know? I've had it all week, just this feeling that I'm going to get a visit, that somewhere somebody's been chewing away at something and something's going to fall over, with me on it. Even that a tip-off would only be a gesture."

"What makes you think like that?"

"I don't know. A feeling. Sometimes the people that come here affect you with what's going on in their minds. You never get anything more specific, but sometimes you get the shits for no reason at all."

I'm really dying for that cigarette by now. Terri knows nothing and she never did, but that's beside the point; I've known her to have these fucking stupid feelings before.

"Well," I say, "relax. This is no useless tip-off. I'm only phoning to jerk Gerald and Les out of whatever scene they're into."

The girl called Lesley reappears from the ladies' room and walks towards me, holding my coat. Now she could do one of two things; she could put the coat on the reception desk and walk out of the club or she could wait, holding my coat, until I finish my phone call.

"I couldn't do that, Jack," Terri says. "You know that."

"Just try, will you?"

"Impossible. If I was to pull them out of what they're into at the moment Christ knows what would happen. You should know, Jack."

I put my fingers to my eyes and close my lids and squeeze my eyeballs about in my sockets. I open my eyes again and the girl is standing by the reception desk, holding my coat. I look at my watch. It's three o'clock. At least five hours before Gerald and Les get back to the club for a wash and brush-up and their breakfast. Now there is no longer any point in trying to give them the good news.

I've done all I can. If the filth gets to them before I do there's nothing I can do about that.

"Oh, well," I say to Terri. "Fuck them, then."

"I believe that's being done at the moment," she says.

The line goes dead and I put the receiver down. I look at the girl who is staring back at me with the same kind of expression she was wearing before she went into the ladies' room. Only this time it's a little better made up.

"Got a cigarette?" I say to her.

She keeps the look going for a few moments more then she dumps my coat down on the desk and fishes in her bag and takes out her packet of cigarettes. She takes one out and puts it in her mouth then offers me the packet and lights herself up.

After I've lit myself up, I hand her back the packet and I say, "Nice coat you've got there. Suits you."

She blows out her smoke and she says, "Coat fetishist, are you?"

"No, I'm a funny one. I like women. But promise you'll keep it to yourself."

"I can't imagine a situation where I'm likely to want anyone to know I know anything about you."

"Oh, I don't know. When you go home to Grimsby for Christmas you might want to give your younger brother nightmares."

That throws her a little bit. "So you're good on accents."

"Better than you are. That elocution's lousy."

Now she's got more colour in her face than she's had all evening.

"You think you're really something, don't you?" she says. "You really think you're something special."

"And what do you think?"

She tightens up her mouth and doesn't answer.

"But you'd still accept a lift with me, wouldn't you?" I say.

She still doesn't say anything so I pick up my coat and put it on and begin to walk towards the door. She can follow me or she can stay there all night or she can wait until

I've left the premises depending on which bunch of thoughts she's having at the moment. I pause at the door and hold it open for her. She's still standing by the desk, watching me. Then suddenly she stubs out her cigarette and walks towards me. After she's passed me by I let the door swing to and I begin to walk down the steps. She's standing at the bottom of the steps looking down the street as if she's expecting a Silver Shadow to ghost up to the curbside and transport her off in the manner to which she thinks she ought to be accustomed. I take no notice of her and turn left and walk down the pavement to where I've left Con's Scimitar. I unlock the door and get in and start the engine. She doesn't appear at the curb so I look in the driving mirror and see that she's still standing at the bottom of the steps, pretending I'm going back to collect her. I stay there idling the engine and she has another choice to make. Eventually she swishes herself round and starts walking to the car. It occurs to me that she'd make a lousy poker player but on the other hand I'd hate to think she was all bluff. She stands by the car waiting for the door to be opened and I think, Why not, let her win one for a change, and lean over and flip the handle and push. She gets in and slams the door and I pull away from the curb.

We drive in silence for a minute or two and then I say, "Where am I taking you to?"

She lights another cigarette and says, "I thought we'd be going to your place. Home ground and all that kind of thing."

I take the cigarette packet from her and shake my head.

"Not tonight," I say. "Got me relations down from up north. They might get the wrong idea. You know what they're like up there."

I light my cigarette and drop the packet in her lap.

"I live off Baker Street if that's not too far out of your way," she says, snapping up the packet. There is another silence.

"How were you so sure about Grimsby?" she says after a while.

"Because I'm from Scunthorpe."

"Scunthorpe?"

"That's right."

"You don't sound like it."

"Well, that's the difference between you and me then, isn't it?"

She says something which I don't catch because as she speaks she turns away and rolls down the window and lets in the sound of the rushing wind.

"Been down here long?" I ask her.

"Have you?"

"Long enough. I think it's a shit-hole."

"Rather depends on the life you lead, doesn't it?"

I laugh and then I say to her, "I expect you think it's all right."

"Have you ever been to Grimsby?"

"Only when Scunthorpe were away to them."

"Up the bleeding Mariners," she says and looks out of the window. We don't speak again until we get close to Baker Street.

"Do you know Crawford Street?" she says.

"I know Crawford Street."

"Well, that's where I live."

I turn in to Crawford Street and drop my speed.

"Just over there," she says. "Beyond the antique shop. The corner where the pub is."

I draw the car in to the curb but I keep the engine running.

"Oh, for Christ's sake," she says and gets out.

I switch the engine off and I get out as well.

The block where her flat is is a postwar piece of architecture, flat-roofed and ocher-coloured. There is an open access to a flight of tiled steps illuminated by dim lights on the ceiling too high for anyone to smash. There is also a slight smell of urine. I follow her up the stairs and we climb three flights until we get to a landing that has two doors and she goes over to one of them and takes her key out and pushes it in the lock, puts her knee against the door and the door swings inwards. She goes inside without looking behind her. I follow her through the door but she's already disappeared from the hall. I follow her perfume and I find myself in a long narrow room divided in two by a five-foot-high antique folding screen. In the first half of the room there is a very nicely restored chaise longue and a matching button-back low chair and there is a sheepskin rug on the floor. The walls are painted Prussian blue and the off-white covering of the chaise longue and the chair and the colour of the rug contrast nicely with the walls, as do the framed, pale modern drawings arranged on the walls with perfect carelessness. The carpet is Prussian blue as well and between the carpet and the walls the white baseboard is gleaming and streamlined. I walk over to the screen and look beyond it. There is an aluminum-and-glass dining table with half a dozen matching chairs ranged against a window covered by full-length gray-and-pale-blue patterned curtains. There are dozens of bright-coloured cushions scattered all over the floor and an enormous picture covering most of one wall, painted in two colours: red and red. The only other furniture in this half of the room is a stripped Welsh dresser but instead of crockery on the shelves there is the best selection of drinks I've seen in a long time. Next to the dresser there is an open door and through that door I can see the corner of a bed and beyond the bed a wall that is just one big mirror reflecting the salmon-pink glow of a single table lamp. The carpet in the bedroom is white and so is the bed cover. Draped on the bed is the coat that the girl has just been wearing, its dark colour stark against the cover's whiteness. Then Lesley appears in the doorway, blotting out the view. But I don't mind that because she's taken off the remains of her dress and slipped on a mohair cardigan over her shoulders, which she hasn't bothered to fasten. She is still wearing her tights and her pants.

"Now you can see what Hume didn't get round to revealing," she says. "Or would you have rather torn off the rest yourself?"

"Very nice," I tell her. "Does Hume pay for the central heating as well? Or can you afford to be out of work with pneumonia?"

"I can afford to be out of work," she says.

"I'll bet," I say, looking round the room. "I didn't know there was that much money in what you did. What was it you said you did?" She doesn't answer that one.

I go over to the dresser and take a glass and pour myself a drink. After I've taken a sip I take off my coat and drape it across the glass-and-aluminum table. Then I sit down on one of the matching chairs and take off my shoes and socks and then I stand up again and take off the rest of my clothes. Then I pick up my glass and take another drink.

"Who's going to win, then?" I ask her.

She lowers her eyes until she's staring at the object of my affections.

"Judging by the look of you, you are," she says.

"Cheers, then," I say, and put down my glass and walk towards her.

She slips back into the bedroom and slams the door and there is the sound of a bolt sliding into its socket.

I stand there for a minute and then I go back to my glass and pour another drink and take it over to one of the matching chairs and sit down again.

"You could at least throw me out a cigarette," I call to her. "I'm right out."

"Fuck off," she shouts. "Fuck off, you clever condescending bastard. You've seen all you're going to see."

Her voice is almost breaking with the thrill she got out of slamming the door.

"You know," I tell her, "I thought I was right about you. I figured this was the way you'd take your pleasure. Showing out then shutting up. Then when you've done that you hope the bloke is going to go raving mad and start tearing off your clothes. You want to be able to blame them afterwards. That's why you hang around with a piece of shit like Hume. You liked the treatment you got tonight, but being a modest little girl you didn't like anybody seeing you get it. And that's why I'm out here, to pay up for the pleasure."

"Fuck off."

"You know that door wouldn't stop a rampant canary. You know all I'd have to do would be to lean on it. But that's what you expect me to do, don't you?"

"You're not having me, you bastard."

"That's right," I say, and I start getting dressed again.

There is silence behind the door. I slip on my clothes and go over to the dresser and pour myself another drink and take it through beyond the screen and sit down on the chaise longue. After a while the bedroom door opens and I imagine her standing in the doorway, looking round the room. Then I hear her stockinged feet pad over to the corner of the screen. First she looks over to the door to see if it's still open and then out of the corner of her eye she sees that I'm still there and almost jumps out of her tights.

"Just finishing my drink," I tell her. "That all right?"

Although she does her best to give me her nastiest look I know that she's relieved I'm still there. Now she can carry on with her games. She leans against the screen and takes her cigarettes out of her cardigan pocket and lights up.

"You got dressed then," she says.

There's no point in answering that one.

"Weren't so sure you were going to win?"

I take another sip.

"The only way you would have won," she says, "is if I'd let you."

I forget I haven't any cigarettes and automatically I begin to search my pockets before I remember.

"Can I have one of your cigarettes?" I ask. "Or is that against the rules of this game?"

She inhales deeply and looks at me and grins. Then she says, "Look in the ashtrays. You might find something your size in there."

"All right," I say, balancing my drink on the mound of the chaise longue. "Let's do it your way."

I get up and walk over to her and take hold of her wrists and carry on past the screen towards the bedroom and as soon as I've got hold of her she starts screaming and thrashing about, trying to catch me in the crotch with her knees, trying to bite anything she can get her teeth close to. At one point she sinks them into my ear and I have to pull her hair to get her loose and that makes her eyes water a bit. She's still performing like this when we're in the bedroom and next to the bed, wriggling and screaming and kicking. I push her face down onto the bed and hold her wrists together behind her back and with my free hand I pull off her tights and with them I begin to try to tie her wrists together. But she thrashes herself over onto her back so I have to straddle her stomach and pin her arms above her head and tie her wrists that way. When I've done that I tie what's left of the tights to one of the rods in the brass bedstead at the head of the bed and after I've done that I can relax for a minute. She doesn't relax but she stops her thrashing about and goes still and rigid. I smile down at her.

"Relax," I tell her. "You're enjoying yourself."

She begins writhing about again so I slide down a bit lower and start to go to work.

It doesn't take long. When it's over she goes all limp and glassy-eyed; her expression isn't all that different to the one on Hume's face earlier. I get off the bed and untie her and she doesn't make any move at all. I feel in the pockets of her cardigan and find her cigarette packet and take two out and drop the cigarette packet on the counterpane. Then I walk out of the bedroom and pick up my coat and go home.

Very carefully I push my key into the lock and turn it and push slightly and then I wait for a while and listen. There is no sound at all coming from inside the flat. Then I open the door a little so that it's just wide enough for me to slip through. I don't immediately close the flat door behind me but instead I go over to the door that opens into the main room and have another listen. There is still only silence. So I take out my shooter and open the door as quickly and with as much force as I can and then I stand to one side and wait to see what, if anything, happens.

Nothing happens.

So I poke my head through the door and survey the scene.

Con is sprawled in my easy chair with his hat over his eyes and his shoes off and a copy of *Penthouse* spread open on his lap. His mouth is wide open and while I'm standing there a deep and shuddering snore rises up from his throat.

Charlie, on the other hand, is lying on the put-u-up which Con has very graciously opened up for him. Con has also draped his leather coat over Charlie as Charlie has rolled his jacket up for a pillow and obviously it wouldn't do for Charlie to catch a cold. Charlie is sleeping quite deeply considering he has one foot on the floor as Con has used a tie to secure Charlie's ankle to one of the legs of the divan. The crumpled bag of crisps is lying on the floor, the crumbs scattered all around. I go over to the divan and kneel down and pick up the bits and put them back in the bag and go into the kitchen and drop the bag into the pedal-bin. Then I go back into the lounge and stand in front of Con and put the barrel of my shooter just beneath his nose. The angle of his hat is such that when he gets round to opening his eyes he will be able to see the shooter and not the person who's holding it. I kick his feet and push the shooter forward a half an inch so that the sight is halfway up his left nostril. Con snaps wide awake and grips the arms of the chair but after he's done that he doesn't move at all.

I let him sweat for a minute or two and then I relax the shooter and I say, "You fucking egg. I could have been anybody."

Con takes his hat off his head as if he's going to throw it but he slows his action up and all he does is let the hat fall to the floor.

"I fell asleep for a couple of minutes," Con says. "Two minutes, that's all."

"That's all it takes, isn't it? Two fucking minutes."

"Yes, all right, all right," he says, getting up. "We all know you never made a mistake in your life."

"I could have made one tonight, couldn't I? I could have come back here and found Charlie gone."

"Well you didn't, did you?"

I shake my head then I go into the kitchen and put a light under the kettle and go back into the lounge. Charlie stirs slightly in his sleep. Con is standing by the fireplace with his hands in his pockets. I go over to the drinks and pick up the whisky bottle and take it back into the kitchen. I drop a tea bag into a mug and when I've added the milk and sugar I top it up with some of the whisky. Then I pick up the mug, go into the bathroom and turn the bath taps on and while the bath is filling up I plug in my razor and start to shave.

Con appears in the doorway, holding a mug of tea.

"Where've you been, anyway?" he says.

"Looking for Gerald and Les, haven't I?"

"And?"

"I didn't find them, did I?"

"Took you long enough."

"That's right."

I unplug the razor and start to get undressed.

"So they still don't know about Finbow?"

I turn off the taps. "That's right."

"So we've had a wasted evening, then."

I get into the bath.

"We will have if Charlie wakes up and lets himself out while you're in here looking at me."

Con takes my key out of his pocket.

"Just locked the front door, didn't I?"

I sink low into the bath and ask Con to pass me my mug of tea. When he's done that he drops the lid on the toilet and sits down.

"So how are we going to score it next?"

"Charlie gives his mother a call, but before he does that I've got to decide which is favourite about what we get him to say. We can either get him to creep round or we can make it, so to speak, a matter of life and death. But first I'll have to put it to those two eggs. If they ever get back from the other side of the looking glass."

"But Jimmy would never wear us putting the arm on Charlie. He'd be too fucking keen to see him put down."

"It's his sister we'd have to get to. We'd have to suss out her feelings. But unfortunately we can only find that out through Charlie and that way's like getting facts from the Prime Minister."

Con lights up two cigarettes and hands one of them to me.

"That Jimmy Swann," says Con. "You never know about anybody, do you? I mean, there's a football team of characters I could imagine turning us in before I'd have thought about Jimmy."

"Jimmy's no different to anybody else. He's faced with it and he's got a choice to make. What would you do? Stand twenty-five for the sake of all the nice people you happen to know?"

Con shrugs. "What about you?" he says.

"They'd have to take me in the first place," I tell him.

Con laughs. "Oh, yes," he says. "They're never going to take you in, are they?"

"No," I tell him. "I've done my bird once and I'm not doing any more."

"Even if it meant doing like Jimmy Swann's doing?"

"It depends. There's some people I'd shop and some I wouldn't. I mean, I'd shop the Colemans, no trouble. I'd know they'd do the same to me so that'd make it square."

"And Jimmy?"

"Now I know, yes. Although I never did like the cunt. He's always been too much of a chancer. I'd have shopped him to get somebody else out of it, maybe, if one of Jimmy's mad moments had dropped somebody else in it."

"And what about somebody like me?"

"The question doesn't arise. You're so fucking stupid you'll shop yourself without any help from anyone else."

Con laughs again and leans across and stubs his cigarette out in the ashtray that is balancing on the edge of the bath.

"That's right," Con says. "There's only one smart bastard in this game and that's Jack Carter, isn't it?"

"Comparatively speaking, yes."

Con gets up off the toilet seat. "I'm surprised you're not floating on top of the water," he says, and goes out.

I stay in the bath for a while, the Badedas bubbles crackling gently in the quietness. The shaving mirror is at the far end of the bath and the magnifying side is angled so that I can see the reflection of my face. The lines that add up to the sum of my years remind me that if I was really smart I'd have stopped running around for Gerald and Les years ago. If I was really smart I could have invested my money and taken my brother Frank from behind the pub bar and instead put him behind a chip-shop counter for a share of the profits. If I was really smart I wouldn't be tonking Gerald's old lady. If I was really smart I wouldn't be working a twenty-four-hour day. If I was really smart I wouldn't be thinking about what I was going to do with my next ten-grand split. If I was really smart I wouldn't need it.

The water begins to go cold so I get out of the bath and towel myself down and put on my dressing gown and go through into the lounge. Con is back in my chair, reading *Penthouse*. His cigarettes are on the floor by the chair.

I take one and light up and say, "I'm going to have an hour on the bed. Do you think you can manage to stay awake?"

"Why do you think I'm reading this?" he says.

"Well keep your heavy breathing down to a minimum. I've got some sleep to catch up on."

I go into the bedroom. The sheets are still crumpled from the afternoon session with Audrey. I bend over and straighten the sheets and as I straighten them I disturb the traces of Audrey's perfume and think about how smart I am again. Then I cover the sheets with the counterpane and lie down on the bed and smoke my cigarette.

I look across at the window. The night sky is beginning to change to deep morning blue. I finish my cigarette and close my eyes and wait for sleep.

Mrs. Abbott

I LET MYSELF INTO the club and the sound of the Hoover whirrs away. The ventilation system is not doing a good enough job of draining away the smell of last night's bodies. But up in the penthouse everything is fresh and full of the smell of talcum powder and soap.

Gerald is sitting behind the Swedish desk. In front of him there is a tray and on it there are bacon and eggs and sausages and tomatoes and a pint mug full of steaming tea. Gerald has on a clean shirt and new slacks and he is wearing slippers but no socks. His face is rosy and glowing as if he's just come off a five-mile jog, like somebody in a cornflakes ad.

"Jack," he says, oozing his phony bonhomie, "Jack. Come and have some breakfast."

"No, thanks," I say.

"If you'd had a night like mine you wouldn't say no thanks. Got to restore the blood sugar. Jesus, we sweated pounds off us last night."

Les appears through the door that leads into the bathroom, letting another gust of soapy air into the room. Les is wearing his silk flowery dressing gown.

"Didn't we, my rotten brother," Gerald says. "Didn't we have a bloody time last night, eh?"

"Not half," says Les, going over to the drinks and pouring himself a tomato juice. "Fucking favourite. And what sort of a night did you have, my old son? Fetched Jimmy Swann round for breakfast have you?"

Incredible. They're bleeding incredible. Facing twenty-five apiece and they're more concerned with their aftershave.

"Yes," I say. "Only he said he wanted some fags so he's just popped out to get them. Said he'd only be five minutes."

Les drinks some of his tomato juice and says, "All right, forget the jokes. Let's be having you."

"Hang on for a minute," Gerald says, picking up the *Express* and unfolding it and propping it up against the sauce bottle. "I just want to see how the Spurs went on."

The front page of the *Express* is facing me and myself and Gerald and Les and Finbow are grinning at the camera in the front-page photograph.

I sit down.

"Better give the sports page a miss this morning," I say.

"Jesus," Gerald says. "I don't believe it. Two nil at home to bleeding Stoke. What a sodding shower."

"What are you talking about?" Les asks me.

"Two nil, that's what I'm talking about," Gerald says.

"Not you, you berk," Les says.

"The front page," I tell him. "Have a look at it." Les goes over to the desk and picks up the paper.

"Here . . . " Gerald says, but he doesn't carry on on the same tack when he sees the expression on Les's face. "What's up?"

Les just keeps staring at the picture.

"Eh?" says Gerald.

Les lets the paper fall onto the desk and Gerald immediately picks it up. Les turns his gaze on me.

"What do you know about it?" he says quietly.

"What Finbow told me last night."

"Jesus Christ," Gerald says. "Jesus Christ."

"You knew this last night?"

"That's right. So would you have done if you hadn't been out tonking."

Les just keeps looking at me.

"And don't come any rubbish," I tell him. "There's no time for any of that."

Eventually Les resets his face and says, "What did he tell you?"

"Nothing, because there's nothing to tell. He knows as much as we do."

"Christ, Les," Gerald says.

"Shut up."

"But, I mean . . . "

"I know what you fucking mean." Les goes back to the cocktail cabinet only this time he adds vodka to the tomato juice.

"Well, that's it then," he says. "With Finbow off the force we're right in the crap. We can't just stay and get hold of Jimmy our way in case we don't get hold of him."

"So . . . "

"So we get right out of it, don't we? We pick up our safety deposit boxes and we get out right quick and stay out of it until Jimmy Swann's put down. And if he isn't we move somewhere where they can't serve warrants."

"But Les, what about the business? We can't just leave it for the first person who hears we've gone."

"Audrey can run it. The filth's got nothing on her."

"No, but they'll enjoy giving her a hard time."

"She takes a third of the profits so she can take a third of the aggro."

I get up and go over to the drinks and pour myself a vodka as an alternative to sticking one on Les's face.

"She won't like it," Gerald says.

"I don't care what that slag likes or doesn't like," Les tells him. "She'd like it even less if we all went down the chute."

Oh, yes, I think, Audrey would be really broken up by the thought of you two doing twenty-fives. All the sunshine would go out of her life.

"Where is she, anyway?" Les asks Gerald.

"She slept at the flat. She said she was going down to the house this morning."

"You'd better get hold of her, then. She's got to be told."

I go back to the chair and sit down and I say, "There's one thing worth considering. I picked up Charlie Abbott last night."

Les puts his drink down on the desk top and says, "What did he tell you?"

"Nothing, because he knows nothing."

"Then, what?"

"There may be some way we can use him to draw out Jimmy."

"You expect Jimmy to come out for that rubbish?"

"His sister might."

"No. Jimmy'd never let her. He'd see her off first."

"In any case," Gerald says, "how do we know Charlie's sister would want to bail him out at her old man's expense?"

"I've told you, we don't. But Charlie is all we have. We can put a price out but that might not be a good idea right away."

"If we don't get to Jimmy Swann, we won't have any fucking time for second thoughts," Les tells me.

"Yes, that's right, Les," I say.

"Well, you'd better get on with whatever you're going to do and let us know what's happening."

"Where shall I send the postcard?"

"Listen, cunt. Just get on with it. You stand a good stretch as well."

"Thanks for putting me wise, Les."

Les downs his drink and tops himself up again.

"So why are you still sitting here?" he says.

"I was just wondering the same thing," I say, standing up. "Perhaps it's the fragrance of the aftershave. Or perhaps it's because I want to know what's all this crap about Peter the Dutchman and some tickle? Don't I get to know things like that anymore?"

"Well, about that," Gerald says, "I was like meaning to tell you. I was just choosing the right moment."

"There'd never be a right moment to tell me anything about Peter the Dutchman," I tell Gerald.

And he says, "Look, sit down and listen to what I've got to tell you before you start hardening up."

So we sit down and Gerald tells me about these four security van jobs Peter's come to him with, all detailed out, all spread over the next eighteen months, worth in the region of £300,000, and that Peter has got a good team sorted and with me on the jobs and Gerald and Les taking care of the money what could be sweeter?

After he's finished I say, "Now look, I can do my bird but I don't like the idea of doing it on behalf of Peter the Dutchman. Christ, you know what he's like, he shoots when he doesn't have to."

"Look," Gerald says, "it won't be like that. If you're worried about that we'll make sure he isn't carrying."

"Oh yes," says Les, "and since when does he tell us our business?"

"Since I fucking run it for you," I tell him.

Gerald says, "Now calm down, calm down—"

But I get up again and go over to the door and let myself into the hall. The morning change of guard is just settling itself in.

I cross the hall and think to myself that if I hadn't been stupid enough to let myself get involved with Audrey I'd have been out of it all long, long ago and left those two cunts to go under in their own sweet way. I swear to myself but there's no getting away from it; I could never risk ditching Audrey, not now. There'd be no telling how she'd react. Audrey's just barmy enough to get her face taken off her just to drop me in it and I don't fancy the rest of my life hiding from telescope artists. So the only thing I can do is to carry on until Audrey and me have salted enough away to clear off where we'll never be found.

Today's guard is Dave Cox, a hardish case from Manchester. Set against Dave's, Joe Bugner's nose would seem petite and tip-tilted.

"Morning, Mr. Carter," he says.

"Have you eaten yet?"

"No, not yet."

"Because there's a couple of big breakfasts going spare in there. I'd hate to see them wasted."

I go down in the lift and out of the club and buy a paper and then I go into the Wimpy and order a cup of tea and while I'm waiting I have a closer look at the front page. It's pretty much as Finbow suggested it was going to be. Nothing direct, almost an air of regret at having to publish the picture, only publishing, in fact, something that could obviously easily be explained in due course. Finbow himself has been quite clever and told the reporter that if he'd had his picture taken with every rogue he'd mixed with in the course of his duty he'd be able to provide the press with an album a foot thick. But Finbow's remark isn't going to do him any good. It'll take more than a clever remark to ease him out of this one.

I drink up my tea and walk back to the flat. This time when I open the door there's no doubt in my mind as to what might be going on. There is the smell of frying bacon and I walk through the main room and find them both in the kitchen. Con is pouring boiling water into the teapot and Charlie is bent double, peering into the fridge.

"No," he says, "there's no fucking eggs in here."

"Why not try looking in the mirror?" I say. Charlie straightens up sharpish and nearly has Con pouring boiling water all over himself.

"Oh, hello, Jack," says Charlie. "We thought we'd do ourselves some breakfast."

"Sorry I didn't stock up in advance."

"Oh, that's all right, don't worry about that, Jack," Charlie says. "I can manage without an egg. I'll have a bacon waddy instead."

"You'll have your bacon waddy when you've earned it," I tell him. "It's time to ring your dear old mother."

Charlie's face manages to turn even pastier than it usually is and he says, "What, right now?"

I don't answer him but I walk through the lounge and into the bedroom and pick up the extension from the bedside table and take it as far to the doorway as the lead will allow. Then I go back to the main room. Charlie is hovering by the kitchen doorway.

"Right," I say to him, pointing to the other telephone on the coffee table. "There it is. Dial your mother's number and all I want you to say is have you seen Jean and if she asks why, say you got something for her then your dear old mother will know you're on the elbow and she won't think any more of it. I'll be listening on the extension so I'll be able to hear what she says as well. All right, Charlie?"

"Yeah," he says. "Sure, but supposing she hasn't seen her. What'll I say then?"

"What you'd normally say. Just tell her to get Jean to give you a ring if she shows up."

Charlie takes his handkerchief out of his trouser pocket and blows his nose, then folds the handkerchief to a clean bit and takes off his glasses and begins to clean them.

"Come on, Charlie," I say to him. "The quicker you do this the sooner you'll be out of it."

Con appears in the doorway holding a mug of tea.

"Well, can I have my tea, then?" Charlie says. "My mouth's all dried out. You know."

"Give him his tea," I say to Con.

"You want yours?" he says to me.

"Yes, give me my fucking tea," I tell him. "Let's all have our tea so we'll all feel nice and fresh and ready to face the day."

Con puts his mug down and goes into the kitchen and comes back and hands out a mug each to Charlie and me. Charlie takes a sip of his tea and his glasses begin to mist up with the steam from the mug. He starts to search for his handkerchief again but I reach out and take his glasses off his face.

"The telephone, eh, Charlie?"

Charlie nods and picks up the receiver and I go to the extension and watch him dial and when he's finished I pick up my receiver and wait.

The ringing tone goes on for three or four minutes and Charlie begins to look relieved. He turns in my direction and starts to make "gone out" gestures but while he's doing that the receiver is lifted at the other end.

"Yes?"

The voice is hard and high-pitched. Charlie freezes in the middle of one of his gestures. The voice crackles down the line again.

"Yes?"

I close the fingers of my free hand and make a fist and Charlie manages to snap out of it.

"Hello?" he says. "Mum?"

There is a silence at the other end.

"Hello?" he says again. "It's Charlie."

"Yes, I know it's Charlie," says Mrs. Abbott.

"I thought you couldn't hear me."

"I can hear you. What you want?"

"How are you? Keeping your pecker up?"

"I said what you want?"

"Well, I was wondering if you'd seen Jean lately. Wondered if she'd been in touch."

"Why?"

"I been trying to get hold of her all week only when I phoned I never seem to be able to catch her in, so I thought maybe she and Jimmy had some kind of Domestic or something and she was staying round yours."

"No, she isn't staying round mine."

"Oh."

"What you want her for?"

"I got something for her. Something she wanted me to get for her."

"What?"

"One of those cassettes. Asked me to look out for one about a tenner but this geezer let me have it at a fiver."

Mrs. Abbott doesn't answer.

"So that's why I want to get in touch," Charlie says. "So could you put me on to her?"

"You'll just have to keep ringing her," she says. "I haven't seen her in weeks. Never brings the kids round these days, she don't."

"Well, can you tell her to get in touch if you see her first?"

"If I do. But I doubt it."

"Well, thanks anyway. Tell you what, why don't I pop round Sunday? Have a bit of Sunday dinner with me old mum?"

"Suit yourself. I'm always here."

"Great. I'll see you Sunday, then. Goodbye, Mum."

Charlie puts his receiver down and I put my receiver down. Charlie stands there looking at me. I walk through into the main room.

"Was it all right?" Charlie says.

I don't answer him.

"What happened?" Con says.

"Charlie," I say, "would you say that your mother was the same as she always is just then?"

"Mum? Yeah, she was all right."

I have a sip of my tea. "Because I got the feeling that she knows that your Jean and her Jimmy's gone away."

"No she don't," says Charlie. "Hell, if Mum knew that she'd tell me, wouldn't she?"

"Yes, that's right, Charlie."

I stand up and put my coat on.

"So what happens now?" Charlie asks.

"We're going down to see your old mother, Charlie," I tell him. "I reckon she'll be able to put us right."

"Here, listen," Charlie says. "That ain't right. You said all I had to do was to phone her. You said all—"

"Oh, fuck off, Charlie. We know you're stupid but not that fucking stupid. You think we're going to let you walk away until we've found your brother-in-law? You think we're going to say, 'Now look, Charlie, you can clear off but don't you breathe a word of this to anybody'?"

"But I wouldn't, Jack. Honest, I wouldn't."

Con laughs and picks up his coat off the divan.

"Come on, Charlie. Let's go and see Mum."

Outside, when we get to the Scimitar, Con gets in the driving seat and I pull the passenger seat forward to allow Charlie to get in the back.

When I've closed the door I say to Charlie, "Right, my old son. Where to?"

"Fourness Road. Just off the North Circular. But Jack—"

"Fourness Road," I say to Con. "Just off the North Circular."

Con pulls away and makes for Oxford Street. The shops are bright with Christmas lights and as I look at the gawpers staring in the windows I wonder where they all come from at this time in the morning, why they're not all at work or looking after the kids.

"What you getting me for Christmas, Jack?" Con says.

"Jimmy Swann's bollocks."

"That's nice. I'll have them made up into cuff links."

"Here, Jack," says Charlie. "Leave it out, will you?"

"Would you rather I gave him yours?"

Charlie doesn't say anything.

"Well, then."

Con goes round Marble Arch and up the Edgware Road. The gray sky seems to get grayer the closer we get to Kilburn. Then eventually we reach the North Circular and drive past the unlovely changing face of London until we get to Charlie's mother's district. It's all petrol stations and light-engineering and cut-price furniture shops and mean tarted-up boozers. The daylight seems to be the same colour as the surface of the road. A Wimpy sign or a Tesco's occasionally stabs out into the different shades of dirty gray but their colours only emphasise the flatness of the depressing streets.

"You want to turn left into Fourness Road," Charlie tells Con. "It's past the Blue Star, just before the fly-over."

Con goes past the garage and turns in to the road that Charlie's pointed out. One side of the road is a row of small bay-windowed Edwardian houses, the other side is a flat waste ground of grass supposed to be some kind of leisure area that stretches away to the fly-over and the factories beyond. Directly opposite the houses there are some swings and roundabouts, right on the edge of the wasteland, but there are no kids playing on them.

"She lives at the end house," Charlie says. "Next to the stocking factory."

"Stop a few houses away," I tell Con.

Con does as he's told. We all sit there in silence for a minute or two staring through the windscreen at the house where Charlie's mother lives.

"I'm going to talk to Charlie's mother now," I say to Con. "When I get out drive down to the corner and get Charlie to show you the way round the block and then drive past here every five minutes. All right?"

Con nods.

Charlie says, "Jack, my old lady . . . "

"Don't worry, Charlie. I've got a mother myself, you know."

Con grins and I get out of the car and the car slides away.

I walk down to the corner house. It has a narrow front garden bounded by a low brick wall and a gate with peeling green paint and only half the house number on it. There is a small recessed porch and in the porch there is a dustbin so full that the lid is at forty-five degrees to the bin. At the side of the house there is a high trelliswork gate.

I stand in the porch and peer through the coloured diamonds of glass in the front door but there are no signs of life. I push open the front gate and go to the trelliswork and lift the latch and walk round to the back of the house. The garden is completely flag-stoned over and is covered with old cardboard boxes full of rubbish and there are a couple of rotting carry-cots and a rusty bicycle frame just to set everything off. At the end of all this garbage there is a six-foot-high slatted fence and beyond the fence an extension of the stocking factory cuts out any light that might illuminate the beauty of the back yard.

I take hold of the back-door handle and turn it very slowly. I push inwards and I find that the door opens into a small kitchen. The kitchen is empty so I slip inside and close the door as quietly as I opened it.

The kitchen sink is full of last week's teacups. There is an alloy kitchen cabinet with the cupboard doors wide open revealing shelves that are empty except for half of a sliced loaf. The kitchen table is about three foot square and littered with crumbs. I squeeze between the table and the sink. The door that leads out of the kitchen is slightly ajar and I push it gently and find I am looking into the hall, and in the hall, bathed in the dusty light that is falling from the frosted panel in the front door, there are a couple of suitcases, all packed and ready to go.

To the left of the hall there is another open door and from behind this door are coming the faint sounds of Radio 1. I cross the hall and stand outside the door and listen but I can still only hear the sounds of Radio 1. So very slowly and very carefully I maneuver myself into a position where I can look into the room. The angle of my view takes in a pale green fireplace with a mirror above it and standing in front of the fireplace, putting on her make-up, is who I take to be Mrs. Abbott. With one hand she is wielding her lipstick, with the other she is holding a cigarette. She has bright red hair and her lips are redder and brighter and she is wearing a chiffon polka-dot head scarf over her rollers and the head scarf doesn't exactly go with her leopard-skin patterned coat. Altogether quite a bright little ensemble for someone in her early sixties. I can see from the reflection in the mirror that there is no one else in the room so I give the door a gentle shove and make my entrance.

Mrs. Abbott drops her lipstick and shrieks and whirls round and begins to back away from me but there is only so far she can go and when she reaches the sofa that is pushed up against the wall beneath the window the seat causes her legs to buckle and she sits down with a thump that makes the dust fly up into the gray light that is filtering through the window.

In a cage in the corner a myna bird says, "Suit your bleeding self, then."

"Morning, Mrs. Abbott," I say.

Mrs. Abbott sits there with her mouth open. She's still holding her cigarette and a piece of ash falls to the carpet.

"I was wondering if you could help me?" I say to her, but she still doesn't move and she still doesn't say anything, so I walk over to the settee. She has a mild convulsion and this time she drops the whole of her cigarette. I bend down and pick it up and sit down beside her on the settee and stick the cigarette back between her fingers. She keeps her eyes on my face all the time.

"I noticed your suitcases as I came in," I tell her. "Off on your holidays are you?"

She still doesn't answer.

"Look, you know why I'm here," I say. "What I want to tell you is this. If you let me know where you were about to go with those suitcases then I promise you, I promise, understand, that nothing'll happen to you or to Jean or the kids or even to Charlie. I can guarantee that because it makes no odds to us what happens to the rest of the family because there'd be nothing in it for you to talk to the law in Jimmy's place. Your family'd know better than to do that twice, wouldn't they?"

She nods.

"So," I say. "What about it? What about telling me where Jimmy is?"

She just keeps on staring at me. The cigarette is about to burn her fingers so I take it out of her hand and stand up and throw the filter tip into the fireplace, then I turn to face her again. The radio on the mantelpiece is beginning to get to my nerves so I reach out and switch it off. The room buzzes with silence and gradually the sound of a jet passing overhead burbles its way into the room.

"Now look, Mrs. Abbott," I say, about to tell her that I've got Charlie outside, but a voice behind me stops me doing that.

The voice behind me says, "No, you look, you mug."

I close my eyes. I don't have to look. I know by the tone that the voice is carrying the kind of reason I'm not prepared to argue with.

Mrs. Abbott is still frozen to the settee.

Another voice says, "Get down on your knees, mug."

As I'm in the process of getting down to my knees the irrelevant thought enters my mind that both voices have Geordie accents. Then there are a couple of soft footsteps and I feel the icy touch of double barrels at the base of my skull and my mind no longer has any room for irrelevant thoughts.

There is a low laugh and the second voice says, "Jack Carter. Fucking great. Just fucking great."

"Bleedin' marvelous," says the myna bird.

For the first time Mrs. Abbott speaks and at first it's hard to tell the difference between her and the fucking bird.

"What are you going to do?" she says.

There is still no answer from behind me.

"You can't do it here," says Mrs. Abbott. "Not in my house."

"Don't worry, Ma," says the second voice. "Keep your bloomers on."

Whatever they're going to do they're taking their sodding time because there are a couple more minutes of silence before Number Two speaks again.

"Ma," he says, "lean forward and feel in his pockets and take out what he's carrying."

Mrs. Abbott leans forward and dives her hand into my inside pocket and I can smell her dry smoky breath mixed in with her face powder. Her fingers close round the shooter and she yanks it out and throws it to the far end of the settee. Then she spits in my face.

"Filth," she says. "Shit. Bleeding shit."

There is more low laughter from behind me. I shake my head but it doesn't speed up the passage of the spit as it slides down my face. And I know better than to feel for my handkerchief.

Whoever isn't holding the shotgun steps past me and picks up my shooter and holds it in his hands and looks at it.

"Jack Carter's shooter," he says. "Beautiful. Something to tell the kids about. That is, if I ever have any."

"You won't," I tell him.

He sits down on the edge of the settee, next to Mrs. Abbott, and for the first time I got a proper look at him.

He has a blond crew cut and the skin around his mouth is covered in eczema. He is wearing a white Shetland polo-neck sweater and a pale gray gabardine suit that is as out of fashion as his haircut. He smiles at me and the colour of his teeth does nothing to brighten up the dimness of the room. Then he balances my shooter in the palm of his hand and with it he smacks me on the side of my face so that I have to roll with the blow and to steady myself I find I have put my hand among the cigarette ends that are littering the grate. I straighten up again and dust my hand on the lapel of my coat and then the shotgun is digging into the skin of my neck again.

"Like it always turns out," says the yob on the settee. "You're nothing. All you clever bastards. You always turn out to be nothing."

Mrs. Abbott stands up and squeezes by me.

"Well, come on," she says. "We've got to get moving. You were late as it is. Any bleeding later and you needn't have bothered coming at all."

"Shut it," says the yob, and Mrs. Abbott does as she's told. The yob looks up at his partner and the pressure of the shotgun is relieved. The yob points my shooter at me.

"Get up," he says.

I get up.

"Go and wait by the front door," the yob says to his partner. I watch the partner go out of the room. He's about twenty-five and wearing a Levi denim suit. He carries the beautiful short-barreled brand-new shotgun as though it's his favourite childhood toy.

"You go and get in the car," the yob with the crew cut says to Mrs. Abbott, "but before you go you can pass me that little instrument that lies there by the wall."

Charlie's mother picks up a second shotgun and hands it over to the yob, but instead of putting my shooter in his pocket he still continues to point it at me, just crooking the shotgun in his other arm. Mrs. Abbott goes out into the hall.

The yob smiles at me and says, "Move it, you poor mug."

I go out into the hall. The denim yob is standing by the front door, pointing his shotgun at me. Mrs. Abbott has a suitcase in one hand and she is turning the front-door handle. She opens the door, revealing a beautifully framed composition with the fly-over in the background, the swings in the middle distance, and in the immediate foreground Con in the process of opening the front gate, his dark leather coat standing out sharply against the yellowness of the Scimitar and the grayness of the background.

Mrs. Abbott shrieks and tries to close the front door but the denim yob pushes her out of the way, causing her to trip over her suitcase and fall to the floor. Beyond this activity I see Con start to drop down behind the gate and Charlie open the nearside door of the Scimitar. At the same time I take into account that I am clear from the yob behind me because although his shotgun is poking through the door he has yet to emerge into the hall. I also take into account that the denim yob is moving his elbow to prime the shotgun.

All these events take place at the same time but the events that follow seem to happen even faster, like speeded-up concurrent images on a split screen.

Con produces his shooter and fires from between the decorative rails of the top half of the gate. The yob pumps his shotgun at the gate but before the shotgun goes off two of Con's bullets have taken him in the stomach, causing the shotgun barrels to be lifted slightly so that they're pointing in the general direction of the Scimitar and Charlie. Charlie, who sees what is about to come his way, screams and can't make up his mind whether to throw himself to the ground or scramble back into the Scimitar and ends up doing a fair impression of a seven-man acrobatic troupe who've just all run into each other. The shotgun blasts off and Charlie is taken in the chest and is spun round so that he falls face down on the bonnet. Mrs. Abbott begins a series of long shrieks and tries to get up off her back but her progress is impeded by the slow sliding fall of the denim yob who now, instead of clutching his shotgun, is clutching his stomach and asking Christ to help him in his moment of need. And in my part of the hall, I have nowhere to go and no choice but to turn and try to change my own situation without suffering some permanent alteration. But I am fortunate in that the yob at my back has decided to back out of range of anything that might be flying in his direction and he's slammed the door just to make doubly certain. So now my choice is easy and I rush down the hall and shout to Con to go round the back and then bend over the dying yob and find some more shells in his denim pockets and restock the shotgun and while I'm doing that I catch a view of Charlie levering himself up off the bonnet like an unfit man doing push-ups for the first time, and Charlie's mother, now on her feet, running towards the gate as if she's trying to catch the last bus. Then I go down the hall and open the kitchen door and then the back door so that I have a clear view of the yard, then I go back to the door that the yob slammed behind him and I shout through it, "You're going nowhere. Come out and at least you'll stay alive."

There is silence for a minute or two. I see Con as he appears in the back yard and I indicate to him that there is the heavy in the room and so Con moves back out of sight to take up a position. Then I hear the small sound of the window catch being lifted. I wait a moment and then I hear the springs of the settee as the yob prepares to make his exit so I barge through the door and brace myself, the shotgun pointing at the window. The yob has one foot on the settee and one foot on the windowsill.

"Don't go outside," I say to him. "It's raining." But he's no intention of taking any notice of me and immediately I speak, his rabbit panic sets him scrambling to get the shotgun into a firing position. I give him as long as I possibly can before the point is reached where it is either me that fires or it is him and in the end, of course, it has to be me. The yob and the window explode outwards into the damp air and I swear and drop the shotgun and go over to the window and look out to see the yob draped over the now overturned carry-cot with Con appearing from behind the corner to inspect the damage. I tell Con to pick up my shooter and I run back through the house to try and at least salvage something from the whole bloody mess.

By the time I get to the front door Charlie is no longer hanging on the bonnet of the Scimitar. His mother has draped his arm round her neck and she is supporting him as they stagger across the wasteland towards the swings and the roundabouts. The street is no longer deserted. Mrs. Abbott's neighbors are filling the front gardens. I run down the garden and through the gate and as I pass the Scimitar I notice that Charlie's glasses are still on the bonnet of the car, face down, having slid off Charlie's bowed head. I run across the road and call for them to stop but they continue struggling on but by the time they get to the swings the effort is finally too great and Mrs. Abbott staggers under Charlie's weight but manages to avoid a complete collapse by grasping a chain on one of the swings and swaying the seat underneath Charlie so that it stops his progress to the floor. When I get up to them I realise the damage to Charlie isn't as bad as it might have been. It's his shoulder and chest on his right-hand side. He must have missed copping the main body of the blast and while his right arm won't be much good for darts any more at least he'll live. So I lift Charlie off the swing but as I begin to lift him I get Mrs. Abbott swiping and kicking and hanging on to me while I'm trying to get Charlie across my shoulders in a fireman's lift. My arms aren't free for me either to give her one or to steady myself so I find myself overbalancing back on to the swing. But matters are helped by the fact that Con has made his way to the scene and he pulls Mrs. Abbott away from Charlie and me and the four of us make our way back to the cars, me carrying Charlie and Con dragging Mrs. Abbott behind him. The audience is still filling the front gardens although no one is prepared to become part of the cast, but in the background there is the sound of the law about to crash the scene.

The yobs' car is parked in front of Con's and as we get to both cars I say, "You take yours and I'll take these two in the other. And get well rid."

"Don't macaroni," says Con. "You don't think the fucking registration's straight, do you?"

I don't answer because the way the last twenty-four hours has gone a straight registration would almost be a matter of course.

Instead I say, "I'll see you at the Garage."

Con nods and pushes Mrs. Abbott in the back of the yobs' car and I unload Charlie into the seat alongside her. Con waits while I get the car started so that Mrs. Abbott doesn't try to get out again and as I move off he dives for the Scimitar as the sound of the law gets nearer.

The Garage

I PICK UP THE phone and dial Gerald and Les's number, and while I'm waiting for them to answer I take out a cigarette and light up and look at Charlie and Mrs. Abbott and try not to get too angry. Mrs. Abbott is looking round the room as if she's paying a visit to her least favourite relative and totting up the dust particles to pass the time. Charlie is half conscious and has no interest whatsoever in his immediate surroundings.

The Garage is a little haven that Gerald and Les have set at one side where they can go to avoid any strife that might come their way. So far they've never had to use it themselves but it's come in handy as a halfway house for one or two of their American friends. Downstairs it's just a garage in a row of garages at the back of a row of big Victorian houses, but upstairs it's been kitted out like a nuclear shelter only more comfortable.

Only Gerald and Les won't be too pleased about Charlie's addition to the pattern on the settee.

Mrs. Abbott is sitting next to him, her arm round his shoulder, holding an unlit cigarette in her free hand. The ringing tone carries on ringing and in the end I put the receiver down and stand up and walk over to the settee and flick my lighter at Mrs. Abbott. She gives me her long look but she accepts the light anyway. Then I go back to the telephone and try Gerald and Les again. Still there's no answer so I press the tit down and dial the club's other number.

Billy answers and I say, "It's Jack Carter here. Are Gerald and Les downstairs?"

"Hang on, Mr. Carter," Billy says. "I'll check up for you."

The receiver rattles down and Billy goes away and checks up and while he's doing that rain begins to rattle against the broad skylight. Mrs. Abbott's ash falls from the end of her cigarette and I have that feeling that I've lived through all this before, even down to the answer that Billy gives me when he comes back to the phone.

"No, Mr. Carter," he says. "They're not downstairs."

"Mrs. Fletcher about?"

"No, not at the moment."

I thank him and put the phone down and swear. Then I get up and go over to where the drinks are kept and for the twentieth time since I left Fourness Road I think about the two heavies and why it was them who arrived instead of the law involved in protecting Jimmy's family. It had been known in the past for Old Bill to offer tenders for something he didn't want to do himself but this wasn't that kind of area. This was a grass and his family, all legal and above board.

So I pour my drink and I turn to Mrs. Abbott and I say, "Who did you phone, Mrs. Abbott?"

She looks at me and she says nothing.

"It wasn't the law, was it?"

She shrugs. "You're so bleeding clever, you bleeding well find out."

I walk over to her. "Why should you get in touch with mugs like that to bail you out?"

"Why not?" she says. "I don't want any more to do with the law than I can help."

"Yes, but they weren't friends of yours. They weren't even friends of Jimmy's. And you didn't meet them at Bingo. So who were they?"

"Ask them."

I sit down again and pick up the receiver. "There's a lot of things I want you to tell me, Mrs. Abbott," I say to her. "And when I've finished on this telephone I'm going to start asking the questions. So while you're waiting I should think about that, and about how I might go about getting the answers."

Some more ash drops from her cigarette but her expression doesn't change. I dial the number of the flat in St. John's Wood and this time somebody answers the phone.

"Yes?" says Audrey.

"It's me," I tell her. "Don't settle back for a nice chat. Either of those two flossies with you?"

"No. Why?"

"Any idea where they might be? And don't say at the club."

"They were there earlier. I spoke to Les."

"So did I."

"What's wrong?"

"Never mind. Could they have gone down to the house?"

"What for?"

I don't answer that one.

"If you hear from them tell them to call me at the Garage, sharp."

"The Garage? What you doing at the Garage?"

"I haven't time to tell you all about that. Just try and get hold of those two fairies, will you?"

I put the phone down and get up and go over to Mrs. Abbott again. There's no more time left for fucking about.

"Right," I say to her. "You're going to tell me all I want to know. The reason you're going to tell me is because if you don't I'm going to start by seeing off your Charlie. Now I've already seen off one mug this morning so your Charlie's going to make no difference at all to my immortal soul. I know you can't stand the sight of him, but blood's thicker than water, isn't it, and you don't want me to prove it, do you?"

She doesn't say anything so I take out my shooter and poke the barrel in Charlie's mouth and pull back the hammer. Mrs. Abbott stares at the hammer, mouth open as wide as Charlie's, then she clamps it shut and nods. I uncock the hammer but I don't remove the gun.

Instead I say to her, "Why the heavies?"

She shakes her head. "I phoned the number, didn't I? The number Jean asked me to phone. She told me to phone her there if I wanted to get hold of her, if I needed to. So I did. She told me to get packed up and I'd be collected. That's all I know."

I give a sigh. She's probably telling the truth. And by now Jimmy and Jean and the kids will probably be well away from where the phone number was. I should have thought of that before I pulled her and Charlie back here. If it hadn't been for Old Bill maybe I'd have left them where they were. But here they are and there's sod all I can do with them. All I can do is get Mrs. Abbott to phone the number, even though they're sure to be gone by now. In this situation there are so few alternatives I have to try everything.

"All right, then," I tell her, "pick up the phone and dial the number and talk to Jean."

"What do you want me to say?"

"Just tell her you and Charlie are in a bit of a spot and you'll only be out of it if she shops Jimmy."

"I won't get to talk to her straight away, you know. There's always somebody else answers the phone first. Now they might not let me talk to her at all."

"Just dial the number and remember where the gun is."

She gets up and goes over to the phone and I take her place next to Charlie. She dials the number and I take the gun out of Charlie's mouth and go and stand by Mrs. Abbott. After a while I take the phone off her and have a listen myself, but of course nothing happens, so after a while I put the phone down on its cradle.

"So what you going to do now, smart arse?" Mrs. Abbott asks me.

I don't answer her. Rain splatters against the skylight.

"Never going to find out where they are from me, are you? Not now."

She goes back to the settee and thumps herself down on it in satisfaction and the heaviness with which she does it causes Charlie to groan but she takes no notice of him. She just folds her arms and glares in triumph at me. I look at my watch. Con should have been here by now. And I'm getting nowhere sitting here looking at Charlie and his dear old mum. So I pick up the phone again and I dial Tommy's number. He's not there but his old lady is and he's got her well trained and she gives me at least half a dozen places I can try. I get him second time. I tell him to call Kirk and fetch him over to the Garage straight away. Then after I've talked to Tommy I try the club again but it's the same story and so I try Audrey again and this time she isn't there either. Fucking Jesus, I think to myself, the fall of the Roman Empire's nowhere in it. So I get up and pour myself another drink and while I'm pouring it I ask Mrs. Abbott if she could do with a drink. She doesn't answer but instead folds her arms even tighter. I pick up my drink and go and sit in the chair opposite the two of them and listen to the wind pushing the rain against the skylight. Mrs. Abbott continues glaring at me and Charlie gives the occasional moan. At one point he lolls onto his side so that he falls onto his mother's lap but Mother, instead of giving him some comfort, straightens him up and then gets out her hankie and wets it and goes to work on the stains he's left amongst the leopard spots. When she's done what she can she resumes the folded-arms glare.

Another five minutes pass by and for something to blot out the sound of the rain I say, "Why'd Jimmy do it then?"

No answer.

"I mean, it could have been fixed, before the trial or after. If he'd stayed tight he'd have been sprung and pensioned off. Old Bill's bread better than ours these days is it?"

"Perhaps he felt he'd rather talk to a better class of people," says Mrs. Abbott.

"Oh, sure," I say, and put my drink on the floor in front of me so I can take my cigarettes out. While I'm lighting up Mrs. Abbott leans forward and with great expertise directs a great gob of spit into my drink, so accurately that it doesn't even touch the sides.

I blow out the smoke from my cigarette and I say, "I've been meaning to ask you, how'd you get so good at that? I mean, it's a real talent. I bet you can get your dentures in a wineglass at twenty paces."

She gives me her smirking glare again and that is that for another five minutes. I finish my cigarette and stub it out and look up at the skylight. Beyond the rippling rain, clouds the colour of lead pencils boil across the sky, and every time the wind gusts, the ripples on the glass alter the clouds' shapes, like a receding tide on seashore sand. While I'm staring up at this there is the sound of a car drawing up outside. I get up out of my seat and walk over to the stairwell and go down the open plank steps and cross the garage and stand by the inset door and listen.

The door is rattled and then a voice says, "It's Tommy. You there, Jack?"

I draw back the bolts and Tommy steps inside, followed by Kirk and his little black bag.

"Hello, Jack," Tommy says, grinning the grin which is his only expression. "Patient upstairs, is he?"

Kirk shrugs his overcoat on his shoulders and stamps his feet as though he's frozen and I nod and walk back to the stairs. Tommy and Kirk follow behind me. When I get to the top of the stairs I am greeted with the sight of Mrs. Abbott balancing on the back of the settee, reaching up to the skylight, trying to find if there's some way she can open it. She only becomes aware of my presence when I walk over to the settee and put my arms round her waist and lift her down to the floor and then of course she kicks and screams and tries to give me a few round the head but I manage to get out of it and by that time Kirk has got

Charlie properly laid out on the settee and has got his bag open and ready for work.

This attracts the attention of Mrs. Abbott who says, "Here, what's he bleeding think he's doing?"

Kirk takes no notice of her and so she starts marching round to the other side of the settee but Tommy and I catch hold of her by the elbows and lift her over to my chair and sit her down.

"We're doing Charlie a favour," I tell her. "So button your bleeding lip."

"Oh yes," she says. "Oh yes. I know the kind of favours you do for people."

I look at Tommy and Tommy looks at me.

Mrs. Abbott eventually quietens down and so I take Tommy over to where the drinks are and I say to him, "Listen, don't ask, but when Kirk's finished I want you to stay here and look after Mrs. Shufflewick and her partner. I don't know how long I'll be. The only other person you let in is Con and make sure it is Con. All right?"

Tommy grins and pours himself a drink. "So long as I'm not here for the duration," he says.

"You might be, my old son," I tell him. "You might be."

I put my coat on and with Tommy following I go downstairs. Tommy opens the big doors and I get in the yobs' car. It's what you would have expected of them. Every ashtray is full and there are some crumpled fish-and-chip papers on the back seat and the whole car has a faint aroma of B.O. I roll the window down to let some air in and I hear Charlie cry out from upstairs so I turn the ignition key and rev the engine and drive out into the narrow alley. The doors swing to behind me and I drive up the alley and turn left and make for Hampstead. I find a nice quiet street in the direction of Swiss Cottage and leave the motor there then I walk through Haverstock Hill and find a taxi and tell the driver to take me to the club.

In the bar there is the usual after 11 A.M. crowd: the swell of drinkers who are all steamed and pressed and smelling of aftershave, and except for the runniness round the rims of their eyes you'd never guess that they'd had to pour themselves a sherry before they could get out of bed and most of them will have spent an hour shaking on the toilet (or over it) before restoring some kind of humanity to their bodies. And now they're all smoothing themselves into a day exactly the same as the last one with the help of Pink Gins and Bloody Marys and Buck's Fizz. The bar smells like a barbershop with a license. And of course Peter the Dutchman is there adding his perfume to the lacquered atmosphere. Today he's all open neck and medallions and suede jacket and cords and moccasins. He's perched at the bar studying the gin and tonic and fresh orange juice he's making a production out of holding. I walk over to the bar and the only opening is next to Peter so there's no way of avoiding him. I should have gone straight upstairs because that's where Alex told me that Audrey is. But as I've also found out that there's still no Gerald and Les I feel like having a bracer before telling Audrey what I think the good news is.

Billy brings me my usual and I tell him to double it and while he's doing that Peter says to me, "That's what happens to a lot of them when they become famous."

I look at him.

"They take to drink. Can't stand the success when they become star personalities."

Billy brings the drink back and I drink most of it and tell him to take it away again and fill it up.

"Mind you," says Peter. "It's quite a good photo. Makes you look quite handsome."

I could put one on him no bother, but it wouldn't be worth the trouble. Bracing Peter would be like having a fight with a damp salad. Not that he can't be hard. Like a lot of queens of his age, he's looked after himself. The hairy chest and the firm jaw and the muscle isn't just part of the package. But against me he'd fold because he'd know I wouldn't just plant him once. I'd keep going so that he'd wish he'd never heard of himself. But the barman brings the drink back and I settle for that instead.

"So what's happening?" Peter says. "Some young reporter down from the provinces all set to embarrass his editor out of his job?"

"I wouldn't know," I say. "Gerald and Les never tell me anything."

"Oh well," Peter says. "It was a nice firm while it lasted."

I drink my drink without saying anything. The less said to Peter the Dutchman the better.

I'm just about to turn from the bar and go upstairs when the bar extension rings and Billy picks it up and then hands the receiver to me.

"Who is it?" I ask him.

"Sounded like Lesley, Mr. Carter."

I put the receiver to my ear and in my exhausted state I imagine I'm going to be talking to Les but of course it's the mad bird from the night before.

"Is that Jack Carter?" she says.

"What do you want?" I ask her.

"Charming," she says. "I'm only phoning to tell you you left a cuff link here last night."

"'Course you are."

"I wish I hadn't bloody well bothered."

"'Course you do."

"Listen," she starts, but I say to her, "No, you listen. You listen. I want to tell you I've got lots of pairs of cuff links and one more or less doesn't make any difference to my general way of life. And the same, more or less, goes for you."

I put the phone down and turn away from the bar to find that Audrey is standing behind me looking at me as though I'm something the dog's just delivered. Now although she's guessed I've been talking to a girl there's no way of knowing how much she heard but she can't blow up right now in front of everybody unless she's drunk. And of course, she's drunk.

"Audrey," I say. "I've been looking for you."

"Oh yes," she says. "I can see you have."

She begins to go a different colour to the one the booze has made her and so before she explodes I get off my stool and take her arm and luckily for me she allows me to escort her out of the bar and over to the lift and when we get there I say, "A bird I pulled last night. She'd been with Gerald and Les before they moved off. I chatted her to see if she knew where they'd gone. She thought I was coming on strong. All right?"

Audrey opens her mouth but before she can speak the lift has arrived and I bundle her into it.

"Listen," I tell her as the lift begins to rise. "We've got more to worry about than some tart phoning me up. Until I can get hold of Pinky and Perky and put them in the picture I'm in dead lumber."

"You won't," Audrey says, leaning against the lift wall. She's relaxed now. All the violence seems to have gone out of her. "Not until their plane lands, anyway."

I close my eyes.

"Les phoned me up," Audrey says. "He was at the airport. He just said it'd be best if Gerald and him went to the villa for a while until everything quietened down. Told me I'd be able to look after things because I'd got nothing to worry about from the law. Said that it'd all be over in a week, once you'd copped for Jimmy."

The lift stops and we both stand there for a while without getting out. Then Audrey pushes herself away from the lift wall and crosses the hall and unlocks the door that leads into the penthouse. A moment or two later I follow her in and as I cross the hall I notice that the chair in the corner is empty.

Audrey is already halfway down the drink she's poured herself. The two half-finished breakfasts are still on the Swedish desk. I sit down on one of the settees.

"They talked about clearing off this morning," I say. "But I thought it was just talk. I really didn't think the bastards'd pull this one."

"So what do we do?" Audrey says. "Are you any closer to Jimmy?"

I tell her about this morning's events.

"Jesus," she says. "It gets bleeding worse."

"I mean," I say to her, "what do I do with Charlie and his bleeding mother? I can't turn them out and I can't keep them at the Garage forever. And I certainly haven't started knocking over sixty-year-old boilers yet."

"We could always do the other thing," Audrey says.

"What's that?"

"We could always do what Gerald and Les have done."

I shake my head. "No, when we go we take everything with us."

"I've got plenty," Audrey says.

"Not enough. I'm thinking of years, not months."

"So what do we do?" Audrey says again.

"I'll have to go back to the Garage. My flat's out for the moment until I find out the reactions to this morning's circus. I'll just have to try and operate from there, at least for today."

"And what about me?"

"You'll have to stay here in case I need you. If we're taken together, that's no good to either of us."

Audrey knocks back the rest of her drink.

"Great," she says. "Just like Gerald. Take care of things while I'm gone."

"Look, don't fuck me about, Audrey. All right? You know I'm talking sense. I've got to try and come up with Jimmy and I'm not going to be able to do that sitting in West End Central, am I? And if I don't come up with Jimmy in the next twenty-four hours we'll have to get out of it before they start making the arrests. Because after what's happened today it's for certain they're going to start pulling in no time, before Jimmy's star players give him the elbow."

Audrey doesn't say anything but instead she pours herself another drink. There's no point in trying to engage her in a debate so I get up and go over to the door.

"If Con turns up, get him to call me at the Garage," I tell her. "And stay sober till six o'clock because that's when I'll be calling you. And if Old Bill calls I've been here all morning."

After I've left the club I pick up the yobs' car and drive back to the Garage and while I'm driving I try and sort things out in my mind but nothing is clearly enough defined for me to separate it and try and apply some kind of perspective. The only thing that is clear is that if Jimmy Swann isn't nailed quick and sharp then I'll have all the time there is for me to do my thinking.

I turn the car slowly in to the alley where the Garage is and I can see straight away that there is going to be no way I'm going to be able to park outside the Garage because although Kirk's car is no longer in the alley, two other cars are parked by the open doors, nose to nose, making it impossible for anyone else to get by. Which is the general idea, because between the gap made by the bonnets of the two cars, about half a dozen heavies are shepherding through Mrs. Abbott and the patched-up Charlie. The minute they notice the arrival of the yobs' car the whole process is speeded up somewhat. Mrs. Abbott and Charlie are hustled round to the open doors of the furthest car and the heavies begin to fill up the remaining seats. I crash through the gears and put my foot down and drive straight for the boot of the nearest car. One of the heavies produces a shotgun and gets between me and the boot and prepares to blast out my windscreen but then he thinks better of it and hurls himself out of the way just before I crash into the back end of the first car. But another of the heavies hasn't moved quickly enough out of the space created by their two cars and is caught between the two bonnets as they shunt together and he screams and the driver of the furthest car throws it into reverse and it backs off down the alley with the crushed heavy hanging on to the bonnet for some of the way until his fingers give out and he slips to the ground like a falling blanket. The nearest car I've crashed into also begins to move off and the driver doesn't slow down just because there's something lying between him and the end of the alley. There is a squeak of springs mixed together with another, higher pitched sound as the car goes over the fallen heavy. The heavy who was going to do me with the shotgun races after the two cars, not even looking down at his fallen partner as he hares past him.

The cars and the heavy disappear round the corner and the alley is quiet again.

I step through the inset door and I don't have to go very far before I come across Tommy. He's been sat on top of an oil drum, his back leaning against the wall. He looks very relaxed and that is because his throat has been cut by someone who didn't intend coming back for another try. The gash is much wider than the wide smile that Tommy used to wear. I look at him for a moment or two then I turn away and begin to walk back towards the inset door, when from upstairs there is the sound of the telephone ringing. I turn back and race up the open stairs and cross the room and pick up the receiver. It's Audrey, and immediately I realise that something is up because she's stone-cold sober.

"Don't come back," she says. "They've been here looking for you."

I know better than to ask who. It was only a matter of time before Old Bill started doing the rounds with his collection box.

"In that case I'll phone you back," I say and put the phone down again. I go downstairs and as I pass Tommy I notice that he's slipped a little and instead of being upright he's now at an angle of forty-five degrees.

I step through the inset door and out into the rain. There is some activity down the alley where the fallen heavy lies. A woman in an apron is kneeling by him looking up into the face of a man wearing a white mac over a shirt and slacks and with carpet slippers on his feet. My emerging from the garage causes the woman to turn her gaze on me and she points at me and the man in the mac turns to face me. The woman says something to him and for a moment he just stands there looking at me and then he begins to take a few tentative steps in my direction but by the time he's started moving I'm already in the driver's seat of the Rover and as I reverse away from the scene it's like the final tracking shot in an Italian movie, the posed trio in the rain as it sweeps over the cobbled alley, even down to the monotonous sound of the windscreen wipers gutting through the damp quietness.

I back into the main road and then I point the Rover east and take the first left turning I come to and for the next ten minutes I drive through deserted streets of terraced houses until I find a pub with a car park at the back. I know that by now I'm only a street or so away from another main road which is handy because the pub is advertising lunch time food and in this kind of area you don't do regular nosh unless you have regular customers, so I won't be walking into an empty bar only ten minutes away from two corpses.

I drive into the car park. There are four other cars dotted about the windswept concrete. I point the Rover at a high brick wall and slow down and stop and take out my cigarettes and light up and stare at the blank wall in front of me.

The rain begins to come down even harder and bounces off the bonnet of the Rover, each exploding raindrop like a glowworm in the midday gloom.

The present problem is to avoid being pulled by Old Bill so that I can carry on trying to get to Jimmy Swann. And to do that I don't want to be dodging Old Bill all round the suburbs. I need a base to work from since I can't go back to the club or my flat. Con's place is out because I don't know where the Christ he is and in any case Old Bill will be looking out for him as well and the same applies to most of my other associates. And those to whom it doesn't apply won't appreciate my appearing on their doorstep and rowing them in. Hotels are right out, in London at any rate, and I haven't the time to work from outside. And as I think about the time, I stretch out my arm and look at my watch and as I do that for some reason I pay attention to my cuff link as it winks in the open light and then I realise why I'm paying attention to it and I also realise that I've just sorted where I'm going to stay.

I get out of the car and run across the car park and round to the front of the pub and push open the fogged glass door. Inside, it's clear that the pub used to be split into two or three bars, but the brewery's done the usual and the pub is all one bar, circular, with a pink laminated plastic top and plastic wrought ironwork making pointless divisions. The pub's about half full and what atmosphere there is is full of cigarette smoke and the smell of damp overcoats. I go to a part of the bar which isn't too close to the hot plates where the bowls of shepherd's pie are festering away and then I spend the next five minutes trying to attract the landlady's attention. She's got platinum hair and lips that don't conform to her idea of them, judging by the way she's drawn them on. When she finally decides to let me catch her eye she shuffles over and looks at me and waits for me to tell her what I want. I tell her I want a large vodka and tonic but I shouldn't have bothered because it takes her another five minutes to go to the stockroom and find a new bottle to replace the empty one on the optic. And after all that business she gives me a glass that is too small to put in enough tonic to dilute the vodka, so I have to ask for a larger glass and that causes an even greater upheaval because she's actually got to take one that's lying in soak and find a dishcloth and dry it and when she's done that she has to go to the trouble of pouring the vodka from one glass to another. And when it's all sorted out and I ask if she's got the number of a local minicab firm that puts the tin hat on it. She looks at me as if I've asked her to show me her knickers. Then she gives a sniff fit to displace her stays and she turns away and reaches behind the till and puts a card face down on the counter and moves away as if she's trying to avoid a bad smell. I turn the card over and it says RELIANCE CABS, and underneath that is printed the number. I look round the pub and see that the pay phone is on the stairs that lead up to the living quarters. I cross the bar and dial the number and I tell them I'm at the Mason's Arms and they tell me that they'll be there in five minutes so I go back to my drink and down it and have the effrontery to order another one which takes twice the time to serve up but that doesn't really matter because of course the cab doesn't arrive for over a quarter of an hour. The driver appears in the doorway and looks round the pub for his client. He's in his late twenties and he's wearing a three-button sports shirt and an ocher-coloured cardigan, with narrow trousers from an old mohair suit. I raise my hand and he comes over to the bar and I down the remains of my drink and he shows his disappointment at not getting a free one. I set my glass down and walk over to the door and the driver follows behind me.

It's still raining. The cab is an old Zephyr and it's parked halfway up the pavement. The driver tells me I can sit in the front if I like but I open the rear door and get in the back.

The driver starts the car and says, "Where was it, Chief?"

"Marble Arch tube station," I tell him.

The Zephyr pulls away from the curb and there is silence for a minute or two until the driver tunes the radio into a pirate station. When he gets to the main road and starts going down the hill he manages to get all the lights. While we're standing at one of the crossroads, a patrol car swings across our bonnet and screeches past us in the direction we've just come from.

"Cunts," the driver says.

I don't say anything.

"Bleeding pigs," he says.

I light a cigarette. "Oh, yes?"

"Bleeding done me last week that one, didn't he? Speeding. Well, I don't have a license these days, do I? He knows me so I reckon he's after a drop so I put it to him and he only fucking 'as me for that too, doesn't he? Well, it's obvious he wants a heavy one, so when I get off that evening I go down the pub near the station where they all hang out and I say to a couple of them I'm well in with, 'That tall blond copper in the patrol car, how much is it to get to him,' and they shake their heads and they say, 'No way; there's no way you can get to him, he's straight. Ask any of the lads.' I can't fucking believe it so I say to them, 'Come on, what's he worth, a century, a couple of centuries, what?' And they shake their fucking heads again and give me the same story, the grinning bastards."

The lights change and he puts his foot down.

"I mean," he says, "you wouldn't fucking credit it, would you?"

I catch sight of his eyes in the driving mirror waiting for some reaction from me so I shake my head in disbelief.

"Yeah," he says. "Fucking fuzz. Take my advice. Never get involved with the fuzz because you never know where you are with the devious bastards."

In the words of the prophet, there's no answer to that one.

The Fountain of Youth

WHEN THE CAB DROPS me off at Marble Arch I walk round the back of the Cumberland and up Seymour Place until I get to Crawford Street. In the daylight the pub is an even dirtier yellow and as I go up the steps in the passageway by its side the smell of urine is just as strong as it was the night before.

I reach the first landing and press the bell to flat number 4. At first I think she's out because three or four minutes pass without anything happening and I'm just about to press the bell again when the door opens and she's standing there looking at me with her mouth wide open. She's wearing horn-rimmed glasses and a black polo-neck sweater and tight white trousers and her hair is pulled back from her face and tied in a bow at the nape of her neck. Then the initial shock passes away from her and she begins to go into the slamming-the-door-in-my-face routine but I'm expecting that and I'm through the door and past her before she can finish the trick.

"You bastard, you've got—" she begins but I cut her off by saying, "I know you probably feel like enjoying yourself and getting all the mileage you can out of the situation, but that pleasure will have to wait unless you want a couple round the earhole. All right?"

As I'm telling her this I walk through to where the drinks are and pour myself one and sit down on one of the Swedish chairs. She follows me through and stands by the screen and begins to open her mouth again.

"All right?" I say.

Her mouth closes.

I take a sip of my drink and pick up the phone that's on the glass table and dial the Skinner's Arms and Danny Hall the landlord picks up the receiver at the other end. "Danny, it's Jack," I tell him. "Now what I want you to do is to send one of the lads over to the club and fetch Gerald's old lady over to yours and I want to ask her to wait by the phone because I'll be calling her there in half an hour from now. That all right?"

Danny tells me that it is and I put the phone down and I have another sip of my drink and I look at Lesley who hasn't taken her eyes off me all the time I've been on the phone.

"Why don't you have a drink?" I ask her. "It's pretty good stuff. Better than what you usually get in a place like this."

She carries on looking at me and although there are many things she would like to say and do she manages to keep herself under control.

I finish my drink and get up and make myself another one and while I'm doing that she says, "I suppose I'm not going to get to know what's going on."

"Came back for my cuff link, didn't I?"

She begins to go red and this time she won't be able to stop herself.

I can't be doing with any of that so I say, "About that phone call, incidentally. I said what I said for a reason. Without going into the ins and outs of it, I had to make it seem as if I didn't want to talk to you. For business reasons. I couldn't phone you back and explain because I didn't know your number so I thought I'd come round instead."

She goes over to the door that leads into the hall and throws it open and starts screaming and yelling at the top of her voice. "Clear out, you lying bastard, what do you bleeding well think I am?"

I down my drink and go over to her and give her one round the earhole that sends her glasses flying and I close the door. Then I haul her over to the chaise longue and sit her down and sit down next to her.

"All right," I tell her, "I'll stop fucking about. I've come to stay here for a couple of days. Not out of choice, out of necessity. And you're going to like it, not because you like me, but because I say you're going to like it. And nobody else is going to know anything about it, are they? Purely because you're a clever little girl and you've got a vivid imagination and I don't have to put it plainer than that, do I?"

She's lost her colour now, except for the spot on the side of her face where I fetched her one. I look at her and she looks at me and then she shivers, just once, the whole length of her body. So now that's sorted out I get off the chaise longue and go through into the dining part and pour another drink and sit down by the telephone and unbutton my jacket and light another cigarette. She stays out of sight on the chaise longue and there is a heavy silence which goes perfectly with the gloom of the wet afternoon light that is drifting in through the tall windows. The silence and the tone of the room begin to give me the creeps so I lean across and switch on the table lamp but all that does is to throw the room's shadows into deeper, darker relief and after a minute or two I switch off the light. I look at my watch and there's quarter of an hour to go before I said I'd contact Audrey. I get up and find an ashtray and take it back to the table and sit down again. There is still no sound or movement from behind the other side of the screen.

The next ten minutes pass even more slowly. Then it is time and I pick up the phone and dial the number of the Skinner's Arms. Audrey answers almost immediately.

"What you said earlier," I say. "About getting out of it. We might just have to do that."

"Where are you?" she says.

"Never mind that. The Garage is finished. When I got back there there'd been visitors."

"Police?"

"No."

"Who, then?"

"I don't know. All I know is we no longer have any members of a certain gentleman's family at our disposal. And it wasn't the law who was dashing to the rescue."

Audrey doesn't say anything.

"So in the light of recent events," I tell her, "I should start getting various arrangements underway. Make one or two withdrawals, know what I mean?"

"Yes. But where are you? I can't get in touch."

"That's the best way. Be at the phone at seven o'clock tonight. What we're going to do might depend on what happens during the next two or three hours."

"Like what?"

"I'm going to have another go at Cross."

"You're out of your mind. You'll never get to him, not after what's happened."

"It's the only way we've got left. I've got to try it. What else can I do?"

"I don't know. But I'll start doing like you say."

"Have you heard from Con?"

"No. But Peter's been in and out of the club like a bloody yo-yo looking for you."

"Oh yes?" I say. "And what would that be for?"

"He says he's got something to tell you, but he won't say what it is. He says he's got to see you personally."

I don't say anything for a moment or two.

Eventually Audrey says, "Are you still there?"

"Yes, I'm still here," I say.

"What's the matter then?"

"Oh, nothing," I tell her. "Nothing at all."

Now it's her turn to go quiet.

After a suitable length of silence has gone by I say, "Now do you see what I mean?"

"But—"

"Never mind the buts. I want you to fix a time and a place with Peter."

"But—"

"What did I just tell you?"

There is another silence. Then I say, "Tell Peter I'll be at the Fountain of Youth in an hour's time. Tell him to take a booth and wait for me. But don't tell him for at least half an hour. I want to be there well before him."

"You're barmy. You're putting yourself right in it."

"If I'm right I am, yes. But the only way to prove it is to test it out. If I'm proved right then at least we'll have an extra direction to work on. Which is one more than we've got already."

"What happens if you're right and it doesn't work out?"

"Then you go on your own, don't you?"

She starts to say something else but before she can get it out I put the phone down. At the moment I can do without all the ifs and buts of what could possibly happen. If you think on those lines in my business then you shouldn't be in the business in the first place. If you think on those lines you'll never have the nous to fix on to the idea that a poof like Peter the Dutchman might be connected with all the ups and downs of the last twenty-four hours, and if you think on those lines you'll never have the stupid face to go the lengths I'm about to go to check that idea out.

I get up and pour myself another drink and think a few thoughts and then I go round to the other side of the screen. Lesley is still sitting in the same position as when I left her, staring at the blank wall. When she sees me, she adopts the expression she always wears when she's got anything to do with me.

"You got a car?" I ask her.

She doesn't reply so I begin to walk towards her but before I can get to her she nods.

"Nearby?"

She nods again.

"Right," I tell her. "Get your coat. We're going out."

"You mean you are," she says.

I take hold of her arm and lift her off the settee and walk her through into the bedroom. Still holding her I open one of the fitted cupboards and pull a tie-belted camel coat off one of the hangers and give it to her.

"Now then," I tell her, "let's make this the last bit of business this afternoon, shall we? Because I haven't the time, I really haven't."

"So I gather," she says, giving me a nasty smile. I let her get away with that one and she puts the coat on and we walk back through the lounge and out of the flat and down the stairs. The rain has stopped and it's much colder than before and the sky is a uniform still gray.

We round the corner of the pub into Crawford Street and a minute or two later she stops by an almost new Mini-Clubman.

"Will this do?" she says.

"Very nice," I tell her. "Managing to keep up the H.P., are you?"

She gives me her look and takes the keys out of her pocket and unlocks the door on the driver's side but as she opens the door I take the keys off her and indicate that she should get in the passenger seat by sliding across from the driving side. When she's done that I get in and put the key in the ignition. The inside of the car smells clean and new and the polyethylene covers are still on the front seats. The gearbox is automatic so I put the stick in drive and pull away from the curb and set off in the direction of Upper Street.

After a while Lesley lights herself a cigarette and when she's done that she says, "I don't suppose there's any point in asking what's going on?"

"I thought you asked that earlier," I say.

She frowns and sinks a bit lower into her seat. Then she says, "And what happens when I phone my friend Mr. Hume and tell him I've got Jack Carter as a non-paying non-bleeding-welcome guest?"

"Nothing. Because you're not going to phone him, are you? Not unless you've got a telephone installed in this little motor."

"So we're going to be together always, are we?"

"Only for the next few hours, darling. Then you can phone who the bleeding hell you like."

As I'm talking I'm taking the car round a left turning. On the other side of the road a bus is just pulling away from a bus stop. Suddenly Lesley throws herself across me and grabs hold of the steering wheel and although she can't match me her action is so quick and unexpected that before I can do anything the motor is halfway across the other side of the road and making for the oncoming bus. She hangs on to the steering wheel and the only way I can get her off it is to grab hold of her hair and pull as hard as I can. She screams with pain and with my free hand I yank the steering wheel over as far as it will go but it's too late to completely avoid the bus, although the driver has begun to take his own evasive action. There is a sound like chalk squeaking on a blackboard only ten times louder as the rear end of the Mini scrapes along the side of the bus. At the same time as that is happening Lesley has opened the passenger door of the Mini in readiness for its slowing down so that she can jump out. I put my foot down and the Mini gets to the end of the bus but I'm still not clear because a taxi has begun to pull out from behind the bus and unless one of us gives way we're going to meet radiator to radiator. I boost the Mini by putting it in second which gives the taxi driver such a fright that he pulls hard over without taking his foot off the accelerator and there is a noise like a bomb going off as the taxi piles into the back of the bus. At the same time the open door of the Mini connects with a Cortina that's going in our direction, moving up inside in the lane we should be traveling in. The driver of the Cortina jams his brakes on and the Mini door slams shut and there is another crash and the Cortina lurches forward as something goes up his arse but not far enough forward to occupy the space I need to let me back into the proper lane and give me a chance to get away. I throw the gear stick back into drive and take the first left turning which is only ten yards in front of me and I wind up the Mini as fast as I can. At this speed there's no chance of Lesley opening the door and getting out so what she does instead is to press herself as close to the passenger door as she can get, but that's not far enough away because after I've taken a few more lefts and rights and made sure there's no sign of Old Bill I reach over and give her a couple.

"Jesus Christ," I say. "I reckon you must like getting sorted. I really do. Jesus bleeding Christ."

I shake my head and all she does is turn up the collar of her coat and sink down lower into her seat. I reach in my pocket and find my cigarettes but I can't find my matches so I have to ask for a light. She pushes it again by ignoring me at first but she only pushes it so far and in the end she fishes out her lighter and hands it over. I shake my head again and light up and put the lighter back on the shelf.

Finally we get to the part of Upper Street where the turnoff for the Fountain of Youth is. I drive past the establishment and then down to the end of the street and then I back into an alley between the end house and the corner tobacconist. I switch off the engine and look at my watch.

Even with Lesley's little incident it's only taken us twenty minutes and Audrey won't have told Peter where to meet me yet so I say to Lesley, "We're going to get out of the car now and we're going to cross the road and walk along the pavement for approximately thirty yards and then we're going through a door and into a building. Do you understand that? That's precisely what we're going to do. We're not going to throw ourselves under any buses or shin up any drainpipes or scream at any passing law or anything like that. We're just going to do exactly what I said we're going to do, aren't we?"

Naturally she doesn't answer. I sit there for a minute or two then decide not to tell her again so instead I get out of the car and walk round and open the door on her side and take hold of her hand and pull her out of the car. I keep hold of her hand and we look like urgent lovers as we cross the road and walk towards the Fountain of Youth.

The Fountain of Youth used to be a greengrocer's shop but the premises have since been done up outside so that the place looks like a cheap Indian restaurant, even down to the bamboo-style neon lettering, but the words and letters form give the game away. FOUNTAIN OF YOUTH, the sign says, and in smaller letters: SAUNA AND MASSAGE. MEMBERS ONLY. The large plate-glass windows on either side of the door have been painted the kind of dark green you get on the windows of betting shops or dentists' surgeries but in the centre of each window is a gaudy transfer of a Hawaiian scene of mountains and surf and hula-hula girls.

I push open the door and a heavy smell of soap and perfume and dust hits me straight away. The door opens into a narrow partition passage with hardboard walls and at the end of the passage there is a desk which prevents the hardboard walls from carrying on down as far as the solid wall at the far end. This is where the clients wait for one of the girls to appear from behind the hardboard so that the membership can be checked out but there is a door in the right-hand partition wall and I push it open and we're in a sort of reception area with a low formica-topped table in the middle and cheap wooden-armed armchairs ranged round the walls. There are two girls sitting in a couple of chairs. The girls are wearing matching nylon tunic-style coats, the kind of thing the shopgirls probably wore when the place was a greengrocer's, although then the girls probably wore something more than what the present staff is wearing underneath. One of the girls is reading *Woman's Own* and the other one is drinking a cup of coffee and smoking a cigarette and staring into space. They both look at me, then look at each other without a change of expression between them.

"Where's Tony?"

"In the office," says the girl with the coffee.

Keeping hold of Lesley's hand I go through a doorway which instead of having a door in it is decorated with a curtain made of thin strips of plastic, then down another passage which leads to a door painted with one coat of white undercoat and with lots of finger marks near the door handle and the word PRIVATE printed in pencil about halfway up. I open the door.

The office is about the size of a small wardrobe. The walls are pegboarded and there is room for a desk and a filing cabinet and that's about all. There's certainly no room for a couple of people of less than average height to lie down on the floor and that is why Tony is sitting on the desk with his trousers round his ankles with his hands under the armpits of one of the girls bouncing her up and down on top of him. The girl is naked except for one of the nylon tunics which is pushed up under her armpits along with Tony's fat stubby fingers. Her breasts are quite big and Tony is fighting a losing battle to keep his lips round one of her nipples as she bounces up and down. And of course my opening of the door doesn't make it any easier for him because the girl shrieks as if she's been stuck in a different place and tries to lift herself off Tony which doesn't do him much good at all as the only way she can move is backwards and as far as Tony's concerned that can only be painful, and he expresses as much by bellowing like a donkey and lifting the girl completely off him and dropping her on what little floor space there is, only even more unfortunately for her some of that floor space is occupied by a deep cardboard box full of Tony's used paper cups from the coffee machine which is where she lands and her shrieks are augmented with the crackling of the cups that make a sound like several penny bangers going off all at once. Tony grabs his injured member and screws his face up as if he's just sucked on a lemon and the girl tries to struggle up out of the cardboard box. She's quite a nice-looking kid, especially from the angle I'm looking at her as she thrashes about among the paper cups, but I haven't time for savouring all that so I grab hold of her wrist and pull until she's standing up, her face inches away from mine and looking at me as if she'd like to fillet me and spit me out for the cat. She bends down and gives me another treat while she gets her shoes from down the side of the desk then she grabs her tights and pants from off the desk top and rather late in the day holds her tunic together and pushes past me and Lesley and sprints off down the passage. Tony slides off the desk and opens his eyes for a second and then when he sees I'm not alone he jackknifes down to pull his trousers up and does a sack-race jump round to the other side of his desk.

While he's zipping himself up and tucking in his shirt flaps I say to him, "Sorry, Tony. I thought you only had a cup of tea this time of the afternoon. Didn't realise you had something with it as well."

"Bloody Jesus," he says, easing himself down into his chair. "That's ruined me for life."

"No," I tell him. "Have a massage. You'll feel right as rain."

I pull Lesley into the office and close the door behind us. There are two tiny crimson spots on her cheeks.

"Enjoy that one, did you?" I say, giving her the wink.

"Piss off," she says, shaking her wrist free from my grip, but I notice that the spots go a deeper shade of crimson.

"What the fuck do you want, anyway?" Tony says, taking a swig of cold tea out of a plastic cup. "If you've brought a new bird we've got more than we need now. Except for the night visiting service, that is. Can't get enough for that one."

"Fancy doing a bit of night visiting?" I say, looking at Lesley. She doesn't answer so I say, "No, she'd be no good for that. She likes it the other way round."

"So what do you want?" Tony says.

"Without going all round the houses, there might be some law round here in about ten minutes' time."

"What?" Tony says, leaping out of his seat and knocking the dregs of his tea over. "Jesus Christ." He runs round to our side of the desk and pulls open the door and shouts out, "Dawn," at the top of his voice.

I pull him away from the door and say, "Listen, this is more serious than that. If any law turns up it's looking for me. They won't be interested in your ones off the wrist. So this is what I want you to do: Peter the Dutchman's going to be here any minute and he's going to be asking for me. Don't tell him I've been here. Just put him in a booth and make sure he stays there, know what I mean? And don't let him near a phone. Now then, if any law arrives don't throw a blue fit. Just throw the switch on the neon lighting just in case they've got smarter recently. I'll be driving by every ten minutes or so. If you haven't switched it off inside half an hour then I'll be in to see Peter. But make sure he doesn't leave, right?"

"Yeah, right, right, but what's going on? Jesus, we're protected here. I mean, this place is protected."

"Not any more. Anyway, they're not bothered about you. But I should clear it as soon as you can."

"Too bloody right," he says and opens the door and rushes off down the passage calling for Dawn. I look at Lesley and Lesley looks at me.

"Good business this," I tell her. "Flat rate's fair and you get half what you make on top of that and, as they say, all you can eat, if you like to make even more on the side."

Her hand comes up to give me one on the side of my face but I grab hold of her wrist before she makes contact and I don't let go again because it's time to leave. I hurry down the passage dragging her behind me. A client wrapped in a towel comes out of one of the cubicles followed by one of the girls, who's trying to hand him his clothes.

"I should get dressed in there, sir."

"But I was recommended to you," he says. "I mean, I don't care how much it costs."

"I'm sorry, you must be mistaken, sir. This is a massage parlor. If you're not satisfied your money will be refunded in reception."

We brush past this tableau and through the now empty reception and down the hardboard passage and out. The cold wind cuts down the street and when we get to the car I unlock the passenger door and open it and give her the keys.

She looks at me and I say to her, "No, I'm not barmy. My hands'll be free this time."

I get in my side and she gets in her side and puts the key in the ignition.

"No, not yet," I say to her. "I'll tell you when."

She leans back and folds her arms across her chest. From the passenger side I can just see beyond the wall of the corner house, enough for me to have a view of part of the frontage of the Fountain of Youth. I pick the lighter up off the dashboard and take my cigarettes out and offer one to Lesley.

"No, thanks," she says.

I shrug and light up. A minute or two later she takes out her own cigarettes and when she's lit up puts the lighter back in her coat pocket.

Five minutes pass by.

Then a two-tone Capri draws up outside the Fountain of Youth. Nothing happens for a minute or two. Then the offside door opens and out gets Peter the Dutchman with his leather maxi coat draped round his shoulders. He looks the building up and down and then strolls in. After the door has closed behind him I tell Lesley to start the car and turn left out of the alley and drive to the opposite end of the street to where the Fountain of Youth is. When we get as far as we can go I tell Lesley to turn right and then to pull in to the curb at the first clear space she sees. And just to make life interesting she does exactly as she's told for a change.

As we sit there in the lowering dusk I remark on it by saying, "What's the matter? Rather switch than fight?"

"You what?"

"Forget it. Just my way of saying you seem to be mellowing in your old age."

"No, I've decided to sit back and enjoy it."

"Enjoy what?"

"The moment when you drop right in it. If I'm lucky enough to be around when it happens."

"You just might be," I tell her. "But I don't think you'll enjoy it."

While we're sitting there, the streetlights flick on and almost coincidentally a few snowflakes begin to drift onto the bonnet of the car, then more and more and within a minute or so the street is full of softly falling snow as it drops on the windless air.

"A white Christmas after all," I say.

Lesley doesn't answer. Instead she rolls the window down and throws her cigarette out into the quiet street.

I look at my watch and then I say, "Let's take a little look. Make a U-turn and drive back into the street where the place is and keep going until you come to the first left turn and take it. All right?"

She doesn't answer but without any hesitation she switches on the ignition and pulls away from the curb. The only thing she does differently to what I told her to do is to make a three-point turn instead of a U.

We turn in to the street where the establishment is and the first thing I notice is that the neon lights are still on. Peter's Capri is still parked outside the establishment. The only activity in the street is the falling of the snow.

"Remember what I told you about the left turn," I tell her, but I've no need to remind her because she's already slowing down to go into it. We drive round the block and she parks in exactly the same place we were parked before, the only difference being that we're facing in the opposite direction.

We sit there in silence for a few minutes and then I say to her, "Going away for Christmas, are you?"

"No, but it sounds as if you are."

I laugh. "Maybe," I say. "But not where you think, my darling. If I go away it'll be to a better crap-hole than this one, I can tell you. Sun, sea and warm sands is what I'll be going to."

"Is that all?"

"Yes. That's all I need. 'Course, I expect you're off to places like that all the time. When you're between jobs. Resting's what they call it, isn't it?"

She doesn't answer that. I laugh and take out my cigarettes and hold out my hand. Eventually she puts her hand in her pocket and takes the lighter out but she doesn't give it to me until she's lit up a cigarette for herself.

"So you're not going up north for Christmas, then?" I ask her, giving her back her lighter.

She doesn't answer.

"Why not?" I say. "I'd have thought it'd make a nice change. All the family together for Christmas dinner. All your cousins and nieces and nephews. All your ex-boyfriends panting for a bit of what you're not going to let them have. Breakfast in bed, funny-hats. Marvelous. Why not?"

"You've just answered your own question," she says. I smile to myself and look at the snowflakes falling in the empty street and for a moment the street looks like Jackson Street and I can almost see Frank and myself as kids running through the snow to get home to help with the tree that was always put up and decorated the night before Christmas Eve. But that thought is with me for only a moment; the closest I'll get to a Christmas tree tonight is keeping company with a fairy called Peter the Dutchman.

"So anyway," Lesley says, "as you so charmingly put it, this place is a crap-hole, and you've made it plain how you feel about your origins, where do you go from here? Because from what little I can gather, there aren't going to be too many places to go."

Origins. The word has a coldness that matches the falling snow. To paraphrase Goering, the word makes me want to reach for my shooter. Origins are the only things in my life I don't care to think about. The old lady fetching in the coal while the old man had his slippered feet up on the mantelpiece. Frank doing his homework on time, his exercise books neat on the kitchen table, his quiet thoughtful knowing surface, and all the stuff about why wasn't I more like him, why didn't I try harder so I could get off the street the way Frank was going to do, instead of hanging around in Rowson's doorway as a prelude to wasting the evenings in the Astoria or the Rex; and of course the beltings my old man enjoyed giving me if I stayed out beyond the specified time. But all that business had made me all the more determined to go my own way, achieve my own kind of success. Christ, I could have run rings round Frank as far as schoolwork was concerned, and he was two years ahead of me. It was just that if anybody had ever expected anything of me I'd had this compulsion to do the opposite. Like the English teacher, a writer himself, he always took me to one side at the slightest excuse to tell me how good I was, how there was no need for me to concentrate on my English; if I just pulled my socks up in some of the other subjects, I'd be six form material, and if I stuck it out in the six form, he'd see me through to university. I mean, he'd just never been able to see that my way of proving myself, of being a peer among my contemporaries, was to show my contempt of the system that expected certain standards of behaviour by behaving in the opposite way, and the irony of the situation being that it turns out that Frank finishes up working behind a bar and living with our old lady and I finish earning the kind of money I'm getting and living the way I do.

But at least he's still living, and thinking that thought I say to Lesley, "I've been to most places already, so with my wide and varied experience, I'll find somewhere. That is, if this business isn't sorted by this time tomorrow."

"And that business being?" she says.

I tap the bridge of my nose with my forefinger. "All you have to know is that you're here with me," I tell her.

"Yes, here I am," she says, looking out at the slow-falling snow. "Here I am, sitting next to Jack Carter, the Fletchers' organiser."

"Well, at least you know that much," I tell her. "Still, in Grimsby you get in practice early, so I'm told."

"I even had a copper as a boyfriend in those days," she says.

"Hardly worth leaving home for then, was it? I mean, it's sort of full circle."

"At least the rank's slightly different."

"Yes, the bigger the rank, the bigger the villain."

"You should know," she says.

I smile to myself.

"I mean," she says, "you think you're so bloody bright— you're making a few bob, you've got the clothes and you're well known, but how bright are you really? Whatever this is all about, it's obviously the end of what you've got, and my guess is you won't be piecing together the strands of your career for at least the next ten years."

Funny you should say that, I think to myself.

"I mean," she says, "how do you get to be what you are?"

I don't answer.

"No, come on," she says. "This'll be the first and last time I'll be on intimate terms with a real villain. I'd like to know, I really would."

"You're joking."

"What do you mean?"

"Your boyfriend's the biggest villain going."

"No, seriously, I'd really like to know."

"You want the story of my life? So you can sell it to the papers as part of your memoirs: 'My Life as a Call Girl and the People with Whom I Mingled.'"

"Piss off, then," she says.

I shrug. "All right," I say. "I'll tell you. Doesn't make any difference one way or the other: I like my work. I wanted the job and I had a good education. Like a ballet dancer, you have to start early in my business, and I went to some very good schools and I don't mean Eton. And at one of these very good schools I met one of the Fletchers' helpers and we got on and later I was introduced to the Terrible Twins and taken on as an apprentice. Since then I never looked back. I rose through the ranks to the exalted position I hold today."

"Except you won't be getting a gold clock on your retirement," she says. "They don't measure time on gold clocks where you're going."

I laugh, then there is silence in the car again.

I look at my watch.

"Time for another turn round the block," I say to Lesley.

Again she does as she's told and again we turn left into Ellam Street. The lights are still on. Except for Peter's car, the street is still empty. We drive back to our little parking place. Twenty-five minutes have gone by since Peter got out of his Capri. And nothing's happened. Perhaps Tony's not managed to hold him and Peter's got to a phone. Or maybe Peter's just out to make a name for himself, by himself, bringing in Jack Carter on his own for whoever it is he's working for. Or maybe, for once in my life, I'm totally wrong.

"Back again," I say to Lesley.

"What?"

"Back again," I tell her. "Only this time park just before the building where the parlor is."

She swears under her breath and starts the car up again, and again we turn left into Ellam Street. The lights are still on. The car's still there. The Mini swishes through the thin snow and Lesley guides it gently in to the curb and stops about twenty yards away from the establishment.

We get out of the car. This time I don't bother to take a grip on Lesley. She just follows me down to the front door of the Fountain of Youth but just as I'm about to push open the door she says, "I'll wait for you here."

I give her a look and eventually she shrugs and walks towards me and I go through the door and she follows me inside.

The interior lights are on now and under the cold neon the place seems even quieter than it did before. I push open the door into the reception room. This time there are no girls sitting in the armchairs. We cross the reception room and go through the plastic strips. The corridor that leads to Tony's office is empty. The only sound is dripping water in the plunge beyond the waterproof curtains on our left, and beyond the curtains of the massage booths on the right there is no sound at all. We start to walk towards Tony's office and we're halfway down the passage when behind us the curtain to one of the booths is ripped back with a clatter of wooden rings. I push Lesley out of the way and whirl round reaching for my shooter but all I find myself looking at is one of the girls carrying a pile of dirty sheets and towels. She nearly drops the lot when she sees the quickness of my movements. We stand there looking at each other for a second or two then I turn away and walk the remaining distance to the office door before the girl can say anything and tip the wink to anyone who might be sitting waiting in the office. I yank open the office door and the first thing I see is Peter the Dutchman sitting behind the desk in Tony's seat. He still has his leather coat draped over his shoulders and in the fingers of one hand he is holding a freshly lit cigarette and the fingers of his other hand are curled round the triggers of a sawn-off shotgun. Tony is leaning against the wall in which the door is set, face to the wallpaper, arms above his head.

Tony says to me, "I'm sorry, Mr. Carter. He had it under his overcoat. I'd got no chance."

Peter grins and says, "I don't just wear it for show, you know."

"The coat or the shotgun?" I say.

"You know better than to ask that," Peter says.

I sigh and I say, "Yes, I know better than to ask that." I turn to Lesley. "Come on. You may as well join the party. You said you'd like to be there." Lesley comes into the office and closes the door behind her, making just about enough room for one person to each wall.

There's no ventilation and I say to Peter, "It's a good job you girls are wearing perfume else this could get like the Black Hole of Calcutta."

Peter grins again. "No such luck," he says.

"All right," I say to him. "Let's stop pissing about. Where are the heavies?"

"What heavies?" Peter says.

"Do me a favour," I tell him. "I suppose you always carry that around under your coat."

"When Jack Carter leaves strict instructions for me to meet him on my own, yes. I mean, we're not exactly bosom pals, are we?"

I give him a long look. "All right," I say to him, "so why wouldn't you tell Audrey what you're supposed to have to tell me?"

"You must be joking. Pass it on to that old boiler? I've talked to women before." He looks at Lesley. "No offense, darling, but you understand, don't you?"

"You're lying," I say to him. "All this trouble didn't start until you went to work on Gerald and Les to stake you for that job."

"All what trouble?" Peter says innocently.

I put my hands palms downwards on the table and lean over Peter. The shotgun doesn't waver and the end of the barrel is touching my breastbone very gently.

"Listen, you fucking fairy," I say to him, "don't come all that with me. You know what fucking trouble because you're part of it."

The shotgun pushes ever so slightly against me. Peter's face goes blank and his complexion loses what little colour it had.

"I must be out of my mind," he says, "passing up a chance like this. I mean, I've dreamt of this kind of situation."

"Yes, you and three thousand others, and I'm still standing upright."

Peter stares into my face for a long time and then he relaxes and his face breaks into his usual smile and the shotgun is pulled back a couple of inches.

"That's right," he says. "I just hope you can keep standing upright for the next twenty years while you're inside. Because from what I hear it's on the cards. And that'll be much worse for you than getting blasted all over the wall. I'll be able to enjoy it every day each time I think of you, instead of for just the split second it would take to pull these triggers."

He gets up out of his seat and begins to walk round to my side of the desk. I straighten up and catch sight of Lesley's face and for the first time today she's smiling, a smile of triumph; she's almost wetting herself at the pleasure the scene is giving her.

But there's no point in dwelling on that aspect of the scene so I say to Peter, "All right, supposing I'm wrong. Supposing I'm—"

Peter cuts me off in midsentence. "Fuck off," he says. "Worm your own way out."

I stand between him and the door and brace him but before I can start to persuade him to stay there is a commotion in the passage outside which consists of one of the girls screaming, which is brought to a sudden halt by the sound of a loud slap. I take my shooter out and kick the door open and the scene that presents itself is of the girl who'd had the dirty towels being held in an armlock by a heavy who, with his free arm, is pointing a sawn-off shotgun directly at my chest. My appearance leaves the heavy in no doubt as to what to do. I throw myself back into the room and to the right so I'm out of the frame of the doorway and I crash into Lesley, driving her against the wall and pushing all the breath out of her lungs. At the same time the shotgun blast tears into the tiny room and takes out the light and part of the doorjamb. Lesley covers her head with her arms and from the other side of the doorway Tony decides to make a break but I push him back into the corner, not because I care about his head coming off but so that he won't be in the way of what I want to do next, which is to fire some shots at the heavy in the passage. I know that providing the girl isn't in the way I can safely do that because by now he'll be in the act of reloading. Which is precisely what is happening when I haul off my shots. The girl has been thrown to the floor and is screaming her head off and trying to curl up like a caterpillar and the pig-thick heavy is folded up in the curtains of one of the massage booths as if that would give him some kind of protection. His head is bent over the job in hand so I have time to place a couple of nice ones, one in his chest and the other in his neck. He chokes and the choke leaves his mouth as blood and he gargles his way across the narrow passage and staggers into the waterproof curtains and tears them down with him as he disappears into the plunge with a great splash. The girl on the passage floor starts to get up just as another heavy appears at the far end of the passage. This heavy too is sporting a sawn-off and again it would be pointing straight at me it if weren't for the girl between, who is now running for the office. I step through the door and pull her to me, the idea being to throw her to the floor and out of the way, but as I take hold of her I feel an almighty thump in my back and I'm flung forwards and the girl and myself hit the floor in a tangled pile. Peter. I've forgotten about him in the short space of time it's taken me to kill a man. I curse and blink and try to get up but the girl is lying across my face and I can't see a thing and then Peter's shotgun goes off and the girl screams and wriggles off me and I look up and the first thing I see is the second heavy on all fours trying to crawl to some mindless destination he's never going to make anyway. The girl gets up and I get up and Peter is reloading his shotgun.

"Don't bother saying thanks," he says. "I might have got some of the stuff that was coming your way, that's all."

"That's why I'm not going to. Saving your own skin doesn't prove anything to me."

"Fucking marvelous, isn't it?" Peter says.

Tony sticks his head round the corner of the office. There is the sound of more activity out in reception, shouting of instructions and opening and closing of doors. Lesley is still in the office with her arms round her head and the other girl has buried her face in one of the booth curtains but it does nothing to smother the hysterics she's having.

"Come on," says Tony, feeling in his pocket. "Out the back."

He runs down the dark passage that is adjacent to the one where the plunge and the booths are. At the end of this passage is all the filthy laundry and a couple of dustbins and a door out into the back yard, and the passage itself broadens out into a flagged square. I step into the office and it's time for grabbing Lesley by the wrist again because it's obvious all she intends doing is stopping there until she becomes part of the pattern on the wallpaper. I drag her out of the office. Peter and Tony are already legging it down the other passage. The other girl is still screaming into the curtain so I swear to myself and grab her wrist as well and try to make it down the very narrow passage with a screaming woman on each arm.

Tony is in front and I notice that he's dragging a key ring out of his trouser pocket as he goes and when he gets to the door he crouches forward and has about half a dozen goes at trying to get the key in the lock and when he finally does manage it the key seems to jam and he fucks and blinds and eventually Peter pushes him out of the way and the key turns first time. Tony can't wait after the key's been turned and bundles between Peter and the door and shoots a bolt and knocks Peter sideways as he pulls the door open. Then from the yard there is a flash, another God-almighty boom and Tony is lifted two feet in the air and drops screaming onto the pile of dirty towels. Then it's as if every nerve in his body is on fire as he goes into a paroxysm of pain and he presses one of the hand towels to what it left of his face and somehow he manages to get to his feet and begins staggering about, bouncing off the walls and screaming until another blast is thrown in from the back yard. His arms shoot up in the air and the towel he'd been holding against his face stays stuck to it. Then he falls forward as though someone's given him a flying kick at the back of his neck.

By this time I'm frozen in the middle of the passage and if the girls were screaming before Christ knows how you'd describe what they're doing now, but above it all I manage to hear footsteps dashing down the passage where the booths are. When Tony got his blast Peter took refuge behind the yard door and now he has the sense to kick it closed as I drag the girls to the relative safety of the square flagged bit at the end of the passage. I push the girls into the corner out of the range of any fire and Peter slides the bolt on the yard door and then we both take up positions at the corners of the passage as it opens into the flagged square. We're just in time to see one heavy fly across the space where the two passages converge and position himself in the office and another take up a spot round the corner and opposite the office. They both have shotguns. Jesus, I think to myself, I've seen enough shotguns during the last eight hours to decorate a Christmas tree.

In the corner the girls are still screaming and I can't stand it so while Peter gets ready to give the other end of the passage a blast from his piece of the collection I get up and give them one or two until they stop their noise. I take up my position again. Peter's now all keyed up to poke his shotgun round the corner but before he can do that the sound of three shots from an ordinary shooter comes from somewhere at the other end, but the bullets aren't flying in our direction so I chance a quick look and I can only see one of the heavies, the one who was round the corner, only now he's sinking to the floor having taken a bullet in the back of the head. The only part that is visible of the heavy in the office is his foot sticking through the office doorway. Then a third figure appears at the end of the passage and although the light is behind the figure I can immediately recognise the shape as that of Con McCarty.

"Get back," I yell at him as Peter squeezes the triggers.

Con leaps like trout and disappears from view as the blast booms down the passage and sets the girls off again.

"You stupid berk," I shout at Peter.

Peter looks at me in amazement.

"It's Con. It was bloody Con you were firing at."

Con's head edges round the corner.

"What the Christ's going on?" he shouts.

"Well, I didn't know who it was, did I?" Peter says, but I've already got hold of Lesley and am running down the passage towards Con.

"Jesus," he says, "I get you out of it and I nearly get halved."

"You'll get topped if you hang around here any longer."

Con trots after us along the other corridor. The fallen heavy is still crawling towards his death.

"Is there a driver outside?" I ask Con.

"Not any more."

We dash through reception and down through the hardboard and outside. Peter hasn't caught up with us yet but then there's a shot and I get the general idea which is reinforced by Peter appearing in the doorway, smiling and tucking his hand gun away.

The snow is still falling. For the second time that day there is the sound of the law getting near to us. I tell Peter the address of Lesley's flat and Con and I run towards Lesley's Mini. Lesley runs too but it's not of her own volition. The sound of the law gets closer. We get to the Mini and Con piles in the back and I push Lesley into the passenger seat and run round to the other side and jump in and reverse the Mini as fast as I can until I reach the left turning we've used so often before this evening. I take a blind chance and reverse right round the corner and I'm in luck so I throw the gear stick into drive and put my foot down and shoot across the intersection and then at least I'm out of sight of any arriving law. I drive the Mini like you've never seen until I've put a dozen lefts and rights between us and the Fountain of Youth. We're fortunate enough not to see any of Old Bill's motors coming in the opposite direction and at least for a while the Mini is less likely to be connected with the activities of the last ten minutes than would a motor like Peter's Capri. Until they get the descriptions out, that is. I only hope whoever phoned the law didn't connect the Mini with the performance and I also hope Peter'll have the sense to get rid of the Capri as soon as he can. And that'll make him sick. He's only been out a fortnight and the motor's no older than that.

For a while Con and I don't say anything to each other and the only sound in the car is that of Lesley sobbing away into her hands. The snow seems to be falling even thicker now and because of the route I'm taking the near-empty streets have all the reality of a nightmare.

Eventually I say to Con, "What happened to you, then?"

"Got rid of the motor, didn't I?"

"Where, the Outer Hebrides?"

"Bishop's Stortford."

"Bishop's Stortford!"

"Got a little lockup there, haven't I? Just outside. Came in handy after all, didn't it? So I parked the motor and came back by train and went round the club just after Peter left for here. Audrey told me what you thought so I decided to grab a cab just in case you were right."

"Well, I was wrong, wasn't I?" I say. "I was dead fucking wrong."

"Now there's a novelty," Con says.

I don't answer him.

"So how'd the heavies get there if you were wrong?"

"They must have had the club staked out."

"There was enough of them."

"There needed to be, didn't there?"

"So what in Christ's name's going on?"

"I don't know. I've got some ideas but now it seems Peter might have something after all so let's wait and see what he's got to say."

"If he gets there."

I don't answer that either but then I don't have much chance because Lesley has wound herself up and she starts screaming at me. The words run into one another and together with the sobs it's difficult to hear precisely what she's saying but the general idea is that she's trying to tell us she's just seen five men killed.

"Yes," I say to her, "and it could have been the other way round, three men and two women, one of which would have been you."

But this doesn't make any difference to her because she just carries on pouring out the same words over and over again and above her noise Con says, "Who's this, anyway?"

"Hume's girlfriend."

I look in the mirror so I can take in Con's expression but it remains the same, rigid with disbelief.

"You're joking."

"I met her last night. So I thought her place would be as safe as anywhere."

"You're at her flat?"

"Yes."

"Jesus Christ. And that's where we're going now?"

"Don't worry. Hume gave her the elbow last night."

"And supposing he comes round to kiss and make up?"

"Then we all hide in the wardrobe, don't we?"

Con shakes his head and says, "Jesus Christ."

"He won't be round," I say to Con. "He's too full of shit to apologise to anybody, even if he wanted to."

I turn left at Great Portland Street and then right and then a few minutes later we're crossing Baker Street. I find a mews in one of the other streets off Seymour Place and leave the Mini there. Then I have to go through the routine of getting Lesley out of the car but once she's out she allows herself to be guided along until we get to her flat. We climb the stairs and she makes no attempt to take her keys out so I put my hand in her coat pocket and take them out for her and unlock the door and shepherd her in.

I switch on the lights and Con follows us in and while I'm making my way to where the drinks are Con looks round him and says, "Very nice. Very high class. I'll enjoy having Old Bill pick me up in such a high-class place as this."

Then he hears me pour a drink and comes round to my side of the screen.

"At least I won't go dry," he says.

He goes back to the screen and sticks his head round it and says, "Is it all right if I have a drink, young lady?"

There's no reply from beyond the screen.

"Thanks very much," Con says, and goes over to the dresser and pours himself a drink and then sits down on one of the big bean bag cushions and props himself up against the wall. I drink some of my drink and go round to the other side of the screen. Lesley is leaning against the wall by the door, her hands in her coat pockets. I walk over to her and she watches me all the way.

"Look," I say to her, "I know how you feel, but try and forget what you saw. It's the only way."

The traces of a smile appear at the corners of her mouth.

"I mean, they came all set to have a go, didn't they?" I say to her. "It wasn't as if they were innocent bystanders."

"What was Tony then?" she asks me.

I sigh and spread my hands. "I'm sorry about Tony. I really am. But it could have been me, or you, any of us."

"Why couldn't it have been you?"

I shake my head.

"He'd be alive if it wasn't for you," she says. "If you hadn't been wrong about that other one."

"I know. That's why I'm looking forward to getting to the people who set all this off."

Now it's her turn to shake her head.

"I once went to the Natural History Museum," she says. "They had the skeletons there of things like you. Only they'd been extinct for a million years."

"Yes," I say, "but unlike them I intend to survive."

The smile comes fully into play now.

"You're not going to survive," she says. "You've got another day at the most."

"Perhaps," I say to her. "Anyway, I might last a bit longer if you're somewhere I can see you, away from that door."

She pushes herself away from the wall and walks to the other side of the screen without giving me an argument. I follow her through and she goes over to the dresser and pours herself a drink. Con is looking at his watch.

"Peter should be here by now," he says.

"He hasn't got a lockup in Bishop's Stortford, has he?" I say.

Quarter of an hour passes by in which time Con and I have a couple more medium-sized drinks and Lesley has another three or four large ones.

At one point Lesley goes into the bedroom and closes the door behind her, then comes out five minutes later and says, "I mean, I can't believe what I saw this afternoon. I really can't. It's like a nightmare."

"That's the best way," I say to her. "Think of it as a nightmare."

She goes back into the bedroom and slams the door behind her.

Con says, "You know, until today I'd never have believed I'd see you row yourself in this kind of situation."

"Until today I've always had a choice, haven't I?"

I look at my watch while I'm talking.

"Think he's been picked up?"

"How the fuck should I know?" I say and as I'm saying it the doorbell rings.

I open the bedroom door. Lesley is sitting on the edge of the bed with her knees together holding her drink with both hands.

"I want you to answer the door," I say to her.

She looks at me as though she's never seen me before so I take the glass from her hand and ease her up off the bed and guide her to the front door and while we're on our way I say to her, "All I want you to do is ask who it is. Then if it's who it should be I'll open the door, all right?"

We get to the hall. The doorbell rings again.

"Go on," I say softly. "Ask who it is."

"Who's there?" she says in a flat slurry voice.

"Peter," comes the voice from the other side of the door.

I twist the handle of the lock and pull the door open and Peter comes in. I'm about to ask Peter what took him so long when Lesley throws a fit, as if seeing Peter has brought everything back to her. She throws herself at him, kicking and scratching and screaming for him to get out and Peter being Peter doesn't like being touched by a woman at the best of times so he calls her a fucking bitch and gives her one right on the point of jaw which sends her sliding down him to the floor.

"Bleeding cow," Peter says, all affronted. "What's she in it for anyway?"

I lift Lesley off the floor and carry her through into the bedroom and lay her down on the bed and then go back into the other room and close the door behind me.

"Nice setup," Peter says. "But what would Audrey say?"

Con looks at me and I say to Peter, "What you talking about?"

"Do me a favour," he says and goes to pour himself a drink. Before he can get there I get a grip on him and have him up against the wall.

"Listen, you've got something to tell me," I say. "Make sure you're able to say the words."

"Come on," Peter says. "I'm joking. Just got the idea Audrey fancied you, that's all."

"In that case have a drink and think of something else that's funny."

I let go of him and he shrugs his coat back on his shoulders and pours himself a drink.

"All right," I say to him. "What's this very important information you couldn't tell anyone but me?"

Peter takes a sip of his drink and sits down.

"After I saw you, I went to Maurice's this lunch time . . . "

"Go on," Con says.

Peter ignores him and carries on.

"I mean, it's been a long time and I've got a lot of acquaintances to renew, you know how it is. So I'm sitting there with me Campari talking to the morning staff on account of there being nothing in the place of any consequence, anything below fifty-first hand, and it comes up about the Colemans and those two bitches having a bit of fun with the night staff. Of course I'd seen them come in but I'd left before the fun started so it was all news to me. So she tells me the whole story and just as she's finishing who should come in but the ex-barmaid who we've just been talking about. She asks the morning staff if Maurice is about and the morning staff tells her Maurice never gets in till one and the ex-barmaid tut-tuts and tells us she's come for her cards because she thinks she's got herself fixed up with something else that very day. Anyway, she says, I may as well have a drink while I'm here and asks for a lager and starts rooting through her shoulder bag for her change. Well, of course she's not in drag this morning and the daylight from the skylight isn't doing much for her frizzy old hair so I take pity on her, there but for the God of Grace sort of thing, and she almost falls over herself. Not my scene you understand, just sorry for her. So we get talking and she tells about how she's been wronged all her life, particularly last night and gives me her version. And while she's doing that she suddenly says, 'Here, weren't you in here last night,' and I say, 'What about it,' and she says, 'With that big butch fellow who's all over the papers with the Fletchers?' And she takes the paper from under her arm and shows me the photo I've already seen. 'Here, are you in with them?' she says. And I say, 'What if I am?' 'Because,' she said, 'I'm certain those bleeding Colemans knew that picture was going to be in today's papers.' Then she explains that after what happened with her and the Coleman women she went and locked herself in one of the lavs and had a private little cry and while she was in there the Coleman women came in to tart themselves up and she can hear everything they say. Your name comes up, about how one of them fancies you and what she wouldn't get up to if she had the chance, and the other one says, 'Yes, but what I'd like to see is his face when he picks up tomorrow's paper, not to mention the Fletchers and Finbow.' And that's what the old queen heard in the lav at Maurice's. Of course, she didn't think anything about it until she saw the picture this morning."

Peter finishes his story by smiling at me. Then he takes out his cigarettes and lights up and says, "So what do you make of that?"

I go over to the dresser and pour myself another drink.

Con says, "Those fucking chancers."

I walk over to one of the steel chairs and sit down. The Colemans. Those bastards are the ones that fixed the picture. And they could only have got hold of it through Mallory. Mallory's in hiding, and Mallory's representing Jimmy Swann. And last night . . .

"So what are we going to do?" Con says.

"What do you think we're going to do?" I say to him.

"Where will they be?"

"I don't know." I look at my watch. "It's five o'clock. They could be anywhere. But wherever they are they won't be expecting us. They know there's a chance we'll suss them, but they're hoping we'll either be picked up or blasted out of it before that happens."

"Yeah, but we've got to be dead careful," Con says. "If we go piling into one of their places and they're not there, then the word'll be out, no trouble, and then we'd never find them."

"I know. We've got to do it right but we can't give ourselves the right amount of time." I take a sip of my drink. "Also, if they're not together and we take one of them out of it the word'd be out that way, too."

"So, what?"

I think about it for a minute or two.

"Seeing as they're both family men, we'll see if they're at home first," I say. "Then if they're not we start looking in their places. That's all we can do."

"Right," Con says, getting up.

"Only you're staying here," I say to him.

"Hang about . . . "

"Somebody's got to keep an eye on her," I say, indicating the bedroom door. "She could drop us all in it."

"Yes, but why me?" Con says. "What's wrong with him?"

"I thought you'd never ask," Peter says.

"Out of the two of you," I say, "there's not much to choose. But I'd rather have him where I can see him."

"Charming," Peter says.

I put my glass down and I say to Con, "Phone Audrey at Danny's at seven o'clock. Tell her what's going on. If anything comes up I'll phone you here. All right?"

Con nods but he's not happy.

"What did you do with your motor?" I ask Peter.

"Left it with a friend at Warren Street," he says. "It'll be on the market with a different colour in the morning."

"Has he got any motors for sale right now?"

"All the time."

"Let's go and see him, then."

Eddie

WALTER'S HOUSE IS A very nice house. Just as nice as Gerald and Les's. It's on Millionaires' Row in Hampstead along with all those other businessmen's nice houses. Only unlike all the other houses it isn't lit up like Blackpool Illuminations. There's not a light on, not even a porch light to illuminate the slowly drifting snowflakes. The whole house is dead and you don't have to get out of the car to know that the occupants have gone away. It has that feel about it.

"Well, that's one less way to Jimmy Swann," I say, lighting up a cigarette. In the passenger seat next to me Peter takes a packet of cheroots out of the pocket of his leather coat.

"They may be coming back," he says. "They may just be out for the afternoon."

I shake my head.

"Walter's got three kids. After what's happened today he's sorted them and his missus out of it. Just playing safe, just in case."

"If that's the case, then Eddie'll have done the same," Peter says, lighting a cheroot.

"I don't know. Eddie lives different to Walter. He still lives in the Buildings, in the flat his old mother used to have.

Like a palace inside, so I hear, but still the Buildings. He likes the security of his old surroundings."

"Yes, but if he knows we're getting on to him his living room and two bedrooms won't seem all that appealing."

"But he doesn't know yet, does he? I mean, Walter's the one with the head, the forward-looking one. It'd be just like Walter to slide out of it in the hope that if everything's blown then he'll know about it when he's called on to identify Eddie."

"So we go and see if Eddie's at home, then?"

I switch on the ignition and let out the hand brake and the car begins to slip away from the curb and I say to Peter, "If we are in luck, and Eddie is at home, you take your lead from me, right? I don't want your enthusiasm for your work cocking up the whole operation. I mean, if it did, I'd just as soon see to you as I'd see to Eddie or anybody else."

"Jack," he says, "you've got such a wonderful way of putting things. Did you know that?"

"I always was good at English," I tell him. "Or so my old English teacher used to say."

We drive along in silence for a while and then Peter says, "Incidentally, I don't give two fucks about what's behind all this, the ins and the outs, but I would like to know, in your opinion, who's going to come out of it best."

"Why, so that if it's the Colemans you can do a little pirouette and end up facing the other way?"

"I always face the other way. Or hadn't you noticed?"

"I only notice things that are likely to affect me."

Peter rolls the window down and throws the cheroot out.

"But do you see what I mean?" he says. "I came to Gerald and Les for finance. That's all I'm interested in. This little tickle I presented to them could see me in the sun for the rest of my life."

"In that case I should keep doing your banking with Gerald and Les. That way you might even get to go on the job."

Peter doesn't answer that and when I make my next right turn I catch a quick glance at his face. It's set like some old boiler who's concentrating on her Bingo card. I shake my head and look at my watch. It's ten minutes to six.

It takes us another half an hour to get to Eddie's. I park the car in a side street and Peter and I walk back to the corner and look up at the Buildings on the other side of the road. They look like reject plans for Colditz. Real artisans' dwellings and I bet Eddie's still paying the same rent his dear old mother used to pay. And with his money he prefers to stay there.

We look at the Buildings for a minute or two more, and then I say to Peter, "What have you got with you?"

"What I've always got," he says. "My quiet little peashooter."

"You haven't got your shotgun stuffed up your shirt?"

"No," he says. "Unfortunately I said goodbye to that this afternoon."

"Thank Christ for that," I say.

"You'd be well out of it by now if I hadn't brought it along."

"If you say so," I say, beginning to cross the road.

"Too bloody right you would," Peter says, following after me.

We get to the other side and go through the arch that opens into the courtyard that's formed by the four interior walls of the Buildings. Apart from tracks of footprints round the sides the large central area of snow is pure and unbroken and under the lights from the landings the whole scene looks like something from an old British picture.

"Eddie lives on the top floor," I say to Peter. "You'd think that seeing as he chooses to stay here he'd at least have bothered to move down a bit."

We walk round the inside of the courtyard until we come to the foot of the flight of stone stairs that leads up to the landings. Everything is very quiet, it being the teatime hour. We get to the third landing without seeing anybody. Eddie's flat is the third one along on the right as you stop off the stairs. We walk along the landing and stop outside the front door. There is a small panel of frosted glass set in the door and through it there is the faint glow of light from deep inside. I look at Peter and he looks at me. I step forward and have a look at the lock. It's a Yale so that doesn't take long and when I've finished the door opens half an inch without making any noise at all. We wait and listen for a few minutes and from inside I can hear the sound of someone talking on the phone beyond a closed door. I can't tell who it is or what they're saying but at least there's somebody at home we can talk to.

I push the door open so there's room enough for Peter to go through and when he's done that I follow him and close and lock the door behind us. We're in a small square unlit hall. Including the front door there is a door in each of the four walls. One of the doors is open about an inch and this is where the light and the voice are coming from. I walk the couple of steps it takes to get to the door and I have a look to see what I can see through the crack.

Eddie's been very considerate because he's placed himself precisely where I can see him. He's standing over by the window with his back to the room, looking out at the falling snowflakes. The phone's pressed to his ear and whoever he's talking to is doing all the talking at the moment because Eddie's just making the occasional grunt of agreement. He's wearing the waistcoat and trousers to a very nice dove-gray pin-stripe suit and on his feet he's wearing a pair of tartan carpet slippers.

I push the door open very, very slowly. Eddie continues nodding and grunting so without making a sound I move into the room and Peter follows me. When we're both in, Eddie puts the receiver down on the cradle which is perched on the windowsill and scratches his head and shoves his hands in his pockets and continues to look out of the window until in the blackness he registers our reflections instead of the snowflakes. Then he spins round and catches the phone with his right hand and sends it crashing and tinkling to the floor. He looks from side to side like a rubbish defender looking for someone to play the ball to, then chooses a direction and begins to bluster through the furniture in the direction of the kitchenette but I take off at a tangent and cut him off and at the same time Peter pulls a chair directly in front of the door we've just come through and sits down in it and takes out a cheroot and lights it up. Eddie now is forced to forget his instincts and pulls himself up short to try and rationalise the situation. He knows there's nothing he can say, because if there was we wouldn't be there. There's no way out for him, but he can't prevent the cogs in his brain turning and turning just in case he can come up with something. So I light up a cigarette and look round the place and wait for Eddie to reach his logical conclusion.

The place is done out like a miniature brothel. Everything that is possible to have a pattern on it is patterned: the suite, the curtains, the wallpaper, the carpet, the cushions. One wall consists of rose-tinted paneled mirrors and yet in the middle of those panels is set an electric fire and round this fire there is even an inlaid pattern of roses. In fact all the patterns are floral (but never the same one twice) and the whole effect makes the ramrod stripes of Eddie's beautiful suiting seem quite spectacularly out of place, like a graph superimposed over a flower study. And then there are the ornaments. There are a couple of shelves on the wall where the window is that are brimful of miniature liqueur and spirit bottles. Then there are three whole shelves on a bookcase that are stacked with mementos of holidays abroad, like pot sombreros or ashtrays set in basket weave or little figures of donkeys in sombreros with little bambinos leading them or cellophane encased dolls in national costume, or models of famous pieces of architecture with tiny barometers set in relevant positions to the design. And then there are the reproductions: Picasso's *Clown*, Tretchikoff's *The Tear*, and the wild horses in the surf.

I throw my spent match in a wastebin with a floral pattern which is set in a mock wrought-iron receptacle and I say,

"I always thought it quiet round here, Eddie, until I saw the inside of this place."

By this time Eddie has reached the macaroni stage and his face has gone as slack as a melting waxwork and the only thing that stops him sinking to his knees on the carpet is the unconscious awareness of the knife edges in his trousers. His mouth is wide open like the mouth of a fish with a hook inside it but he's not going to be able to control his lips so that he can form any words. His face is the colour of vanilla ice cream and beads of oily sweat are slowly following the downward pattern of his expression. Inside he must be wishing he'd worshiped a little more fastidiously at the shrine of the God he's now praying to.

"Well," I say. "Eddie."

Eddie's hands move briefly as though somebody's pulling the strings and I walk over to him and flip the top of my cigarette packet and offer him a cigarette but all that happens is that his mouth falls open a little bit wider. So I take hold of one of his hands and insert a cigarette between the fore and middle fingers and lift his arm and hold his hand so that the cigarette is near his lips and he automatically does the rest himself. I light the cigarette for him and he manages to inhale and while he's doing that I draw well back and hit him as hard as I can just below his breastbone. The punch makes him stagger backwards rather than fall over immediately but he's got to fall over sometime and when he does it's across a low table next to the colour telly, upending the little wrought-iron magazine holder and scattering the telly papers all over the place. I give him a few minutes to get his breath back and to pass the time I watch the cigarette I gave him burn a hole in the centre of one of the flowers in the pattern on the carpet.

When Eddie's got himself back together I say to him, "As you know, we haven't the time to play mulberry bushes. All we want to know is what's happening, from beginning to end. That's all we want, Eddie, and I think you know that shooting shit won't help your position one little bit."

Eddie drags himself up off the floor and supports himself on the back of an easy chair and exercises his lungs for a couple of minutes.

Then he looks up at me and says, "What's going to happen to me?"

"I don't know, Eddie," I tell him.

He looks down at the back of the chair again and nods.

"Yes," he says.

I sit down in the opposite armchair and say, "Tell us first, Eddie. You never know, depending on what kind of fairy tale it is there might just be a happy ending."

Eddie stays the way he is for a minute then works his way round to the front of the chair and eases himself down into it. Then he sees the cigarette lying on the floor burning its way through the carpet and he bends over and picks it up and flicks the ash into an ashtray and takes a drag.

Then he passes his hand through his hair and is about to speak, but before he can, I say, "First, Eddie. The wife. The kids. Where are they?"

"They're out of it," he says. "They're away. That I'm not telling you."

"It's not important right now," I tell him. "Just didn't want us to be interrupted once you got into full flow."

Eddie takes another drag on his cigarette.

"It wasn't my idea," he says.

I don't make any comment on his statement so there's no alternative but for him to go on. "I mean, I said to Wally, 'We're all right as we are, aren't we? What's wrong with the setup we already have? This idea is going to bring us nothing but fucking strife.' But Wally just rubbed his hands together and said he'd been looking forward to a setup like this for years."

Eddie puts the cigarette out in the ashtray. He looks at me and then at Peter and then back to me.

"What was the idea, Eddie?" I say to him.

"Well, it wasn't even Wally's idea, was it? I mean, if it hadn't been served up to him he'd never have thought of it by himself, would he? I mean, be fair. Would he?"

"So whose idea was it?"

Eddie makes sure he's not looking into my eyes when he says, "Hume."

Eddie might be avoiding my eyes but I can certainly feel Peter's boring into the back of my neck when the word drops into the silence of the room.

"See, Hume comes round to see Wally one day about this bullion job we put out over in Bromley. He comes steaming in with his usual spiel about how he's fitted up somebody who wasn't even on the job and how to save himself ten out of twenty this somebody's going to stand up and point at me and Wally. Of course, Wally tells Hume to piss off and go and play in the next street. I mean, the thing is that this somebody's a geezer called Danny Ross and Wally did Danny a great big favour once and Danny's soft as shit and he'd do thirty rather than point at me and Wally and Wally tells Hume as much. Hume doesn't like it, understandably enough, so he takes his pleasure by saying that if Danny's such an old mucker of ours we'll enjoy seeing him do a twenty-five for this and a couple of others Hume will fit him in on, not to mention Danny's old lady who he'll do for harbouring and receiving and being an accessory and all that rubbish. So Walter says all right, all right, how much? Hume calms down and then he asks us how much we fenced it for. I mean, he sat there and fucking asked us. So Walter tells him half of what we got for it and Hume says in that case ten grand'll see Danny at home with his wife and kiddies until the next time. Wally says five and they finally fix a figure. And with that Hume trolleys off. For a while Wally's blazing and all for putting a bomb outside Hume's front door but I cool him off and he lets the matter drop. Then a month or so later Hume comes back and says to us how'd we like to have him as a permanent partner? Wally says fucking lovely, it'll only cost us fifty grand a year at Hume's rates, why doesn't he start today? Hume wears it all and when Wally's finished he says, 'Let's not be silly, you couldn't even afford that if you had Gerald and Les's patch as well,' and Wally says, 'Yes, you can afford anything when you're dead.' Hume shakes his head a few times and then puts us this proposition; first, that he'd heard he could get Finbow's job if Finbow was out of it. And that would be a step in the right direction but Gerald and Les would still be there, Finbow or not. So, he says, supposing somebody blew the whistle on Gerald and Les? Supposing it could be guaranteed that somebody would be out of the country the day the trial ended, with a new name on his passport and free passage to anywhere he wants to go with his family and ten thousand quid out of the police fund? Plus, of course, whatever me and Wally'd want to chip in, which could make the offer much more attractive. And he says with him in West End Central and Gerald and Les and you out of the way he'd look after us the way Finbow looked after you lot. And we'd be doing twice the business, what with the shops and the clubs and the places and all those things."

"Yes," I say to him. "I know about those things, Eddie."

"Look, Jack, for Christ's sake, do me a favour, will you?" He slides off the chair and sinks to the floor and puts his hands on my knees. "Christ, I didn't . . . "

I take his hands away.

"Sit down and finish the story," I say to him. "There's time for all that afterwards." Eddie shakes his head and a tear flicks from his eye on to the carpet but he back-pedals on his knees and finds the chair and slides back into it.

"I told Wally he'd be barmy to think of it but Wally shut me up and asked Hume if he'd worked out how to do it yet. Hume said he'd let us know and he went away. He comes back a week later and tells us he's done some sniffing and he's found out from someone in the Fraud Squad that Mallory's behind some dodgy companies that are just about to make the headlines and even Mallory won't be able to avoid getting five to seven. So he promises Mallory some friendship if he can figure a way to blow Finbow and put it on Gerald and Les. And he does. He comes up with the pictures and Jimmy Swann. Wally's over the moon about it, especially as Hume says he's already put it to the top brass and they're prepared to let him play it his way and also finance Jimmy. And from then on there's no stopping Wally. He can't wait for the action to start."

"What held him back last night?"

"Hume wanted him to keep buttoned up. But today when Wally heard about you getting to the Abbotts he decided to have his fun and join in. You know what Wally's like."

"Yes, I know what Wally's like," I say. I light another cigarette. "But Hume saw me last night. He could have had me then. Jimmy needn't even have signed his statement."

"Hume fixed Finbow but he doesn't want anybody to know on account of being next in line. So he's worked it that someone else does the lifting and he's prepared to come in with any further names and evidence for the glory later on; that's why so many names are still walking around enjoying the fresh air. But after today Hume will have to start pulling them in right away."

Eddie stops talking. I don't say anything for a while. Eventually I say, "So where's Jimmy Swann?"

Eddie shakes his head. "Only Hume knows that."

I look at him. "I'll only ask you once more, Eddie."

"Jack, honest. I don't know. Christ, I'd tell you if I knew. I've told you everything else. Why shouldn't I tell you that?"

"All right, we'll leave that for the time being. So where's Walter?"

He shakes his head again.

"Come on, Eddie," I say to him. "You know where Walter is."

"Yes," he says. "I know where he is. But Jack, he's my own brother. How can I tell you where my own brother is?"

"Quite easily," I tell him, and wait for the reply.

After a while Eddie says, "Wally's got this place in Suffolk. Big old farmhouse in about ten acres. Bought it last year and had it done up. He went there this afternoon. He's staying till Boxing Day."

I sit there and think about what Eddie's told me. Then I say, "All right, Eddie. Put your coat on."

"Jack . . . " Eddie says.

"Your coat."

Eddie's face sags even more and he drags himself up out of his chair and I get up as well.

"Hang on a minute, Jack," Peter says from behind me. "Don't you think we ought to have a chat before we do anything we can't go back on?"

I turn round and look at Peter. He's still lounging in the chair by the door but now he's got his shooter resting in his lap. He's holding it, and although he's extremely careful that it shouldn't be pointing directly in my direction, it wouldn't take much if the situation made that eventuality necessary.

"I mean," Peter says, "it bears thinking about, doesn't it?"

"Oh yes?" I say.

"Well, look at it this way," he says. "What's the point in plowing on against all the odds? If what Eddie says is right, Hume has got it all sewn up. There's no going back. Gerald and Les are finished."

I don't say anything.

From behind me Eddie says, "That's right. They're finished. They can't come back now."

I turn to face Eddie. He's standing there with his face all lit up, thinking he can see a way out of his situation.

"Get your coat, Eddie," I tell him.

Eddie looks at Peter and I follow his glance.

Peter says, "We could do a deal with Hume. We could tell him where to get at Gerald and Les and make the takeover nice and smooth in return for being left out of it and carrying on as we are."

"That's right," Eddie says. "Wally's always wanted you on the firm, Jack. It'd work out perfect."

"And you could still get the finance for your tickle," I say to Peter.

"Spot on," he says. "You got it in one."

"Except that if we were to do what you've just said we'd both be on twenty-fives whatever this chancer's trying to tell us."

"You wouldn't," Eddie says. "I guarantee it. I can phone Hume and do a deal right now."

"Do you believe what Eddie says?" I ask Peter. Peter shrugs.

"What's the alternative?" he says. "We're on a definite loser the other way."

"And what if I say I'm going to play this the way I set out to play it?"

Peter looks me in the face and is quite motionless. This is where he has to decide what to do and until he's done that he is very careful not to do anything which will cause me to react. He looks beyond me at Eddie and then back to me and he's just about to speak when there is a slight movement behind me and I whirl round just in time to see Eddie disappearing round the corner of the L-shaped room, the part that leads to the kitchenette. I rush after him but there is a lot of furniture in the way and before I'm at the corner of the L the kitchenette door has slammed. Peter is already on his feet and I shout at him to open the door behind the chair he was sitting in and get into the hall. I make it to the kitchenette door and yank it open but of course Eddie is no longer in the kitchenette because through its other door, the one that leads into the hall, I can see Eddie scrambling at the lock handle of the outside door. I hurry across the kitchenette but I'm never going to make it because now Eddie has got the outside door open and the only thing that's going to stop him is Peter but the outside door slams as Peter appears in the hall. I get into the hall a second after Peter and already he's twisting the lock handle. He's gripping his shooter in his free hand.

"Whatever you do, you cunt, don't shoot," I tell him as I follow him through the door. We turn left but there's no sign of Eddie; he's already legging it down the stairs. We rush along the landing and Peter calls Eddie's name as we go, as if that's going to make him stop for a moment's reflection. I make it to the top of the stairs first and start going down them two at a time but when I get to the second landing I'm still no closer to Eddie because he's already out of sight and on the second flight of stairs but when I get to the top of them I stop short when I see what's on the third step down: one of Eddie's tartan slippers is lying there, sole upwards, and I look beyond the slipper to the foot of the stone staircase and see the still figure of Eddie lying there, arms outstretched, face down, his head at a completely wrong angle to the rest of his body. He'd tripped and broken his neck.

Peter pulls up sharp too and we both stand there at the top of the stairs looking down at Eddie's body. Then I turn to Peter and take hold of him by his neck and with all the angry force in my body I push him backwards until the balcony wall stops us going any farther. The shooter slips out of Peter's fingers and with both hands he tries to loosen my grip on his neck but there's no way he's going to be able to manage that. I keep pressing until he's leaning out over the empty courtyard and with my free hand I hit him several times across the face.

"I should let you drop," I tell him. "I should let you drop right now."

I hit him again and step back and then I pick up his shooter and point it at him.

"Or shall I shoot your fucking kneecaps off? Shall I do that instead?"

Peter pushes himself away from the balcony wall and looks at me the way Eddie had looked at me when I'd first walked into his living room.

"Jack . . . " he says.

"Shut it," I tell him. "Another word and I'll do it."

Then I put his shooter in my pocket and turn away from him and begin to walk down the stairs, picking up Eddie's slipper on the way. When I get to Eddie, I bend over him and turn him face upwards but there are no miracles for Eddie this Christmas. His dead eyes reflect the naked light bulb in the stairwell's ceiling.

Peter makes his way down to the bottom of the steps and leans against the wall, supporting himself on the handrail. I look up at him.

"All right, you fucking egg," I tell him. "Get hold of the legs."

I put the slipper back on Eddie's foot and then I take hold of him underneath his armpits and look up at Peter again and he moves and gets hold of the legs and as we lift, some change slips out of Eddie's trouser pocket and the coins make a tinkling sound as they hit the stone floor.

We get Eddie to the bottom of the stairs that open into the courtyard. The snow is still falling and the courtyard is still empty. We carry Eddie away from the light on the staircase and into the shadow of the balcony above and then we put Eddie down.

"Right," I say to Peter. "Now you go and fetch the car and back it in the courtyard entrance and open up the boot. I know you're going to do exactly that because you don't want to wake up every night for the rest of your life wondering if tonight's the night I'm going to appear at the end of your bedstead. Do you?"

I hand him the car keys. He doesn't answer. He looks at me for a moment and turns away and hurries across to the courtyard entrance and disappears round the corner. Then I take hold of Eddie again and under cover of the balcony I drag him round to the arch and wait for Peter. I look at my watch and decide to give him two minutes. If he's not back by then the only thing I can do is leave Eddie where he is and take one of the few remaining chances I have left.

But within the allowed time there is the sound of the car backing into the archway. I grab Eddie again and start pulling him through the snow and I hear Peter get out of the car and unlock the boot and by that time I have got Eddie to the rear of the car. Peter takes Eddie's legs again and we lift Eddie into the boot and close the lid. Then I tell Peter to drive the car back to where it was before and wait and I go back up to Eddie's flat and put the furniture back the way it was and get rid of the cigarette ends and then I pick up the address book that Eddie had been writing in and slip it in my pocket. After I've done that I put the flat black case on the settee and flip the catches and open the lid and my eyes are greeted with the beautifully symmetrical pattern of ranks of wads of nice crisp notes. At a quick guess I would say there is twenty thousand worth at least. I look into the case for a moment or two and then I get up and find Eddie's bedroom and slide open one of the doors on the built-in wardrobe. I take out one of Eddie's overcoats and a pair of his shoes and as I'm doing that I notice that on the top shelf there is a stack of brightly wrapped Christmas presents out of sight and of reach, all ready for Eddie to deliver to wherever his wife and kids are spending Christmas.

I shut up the wardrobe and then I switch out all the lights and close all the doors and go out of the flat.

When I get back to where Peter is I throw the coat and the shoes in the back seat and tell him to drive to a place I know beyond Liverpool Street. Peter does as he's told and sets off without saying anything. His face looks even pastier under the sodium streetlighting and his mouth is set in a light thin line and it's not because he's been affected by Eddie's death because normally he'd be making the most of the funny side of it. I sit there in silence myself and let him sweat for a while.

The place I'm thinking of is about half a mile off Liverpool Street itself. This place used to be a block of insurance offices and for the last few weeks it's been in the process of being demolished. I passed by it a few days ago and its cellars and their interlocking passages are now wide open to the weather. It takes us about quarter of an hour to get there and when we arrive I tell Peter to drive down a side street that would have been boundaried by one of the walls of the demolished building. We park at the far corner of the site away from any lights, and I tell Peter to wait in the car while I go and take a look around. I walk onto the site and over to the edge of one of the sunken corridors and drop down into it. Now I'm out of sight and I take out my key ring and play the small torch along the corridor until I come to a pile of plastic rubble sacks lying on the floor next to a narrow cupboard set in a tiled wall. I climb out of the corridor and go back to the car and tell Peter to get out and open up the boot and we carry Eddie back to the corridor and I get down in it and Peter lowers Eddie down onto my shoulders and I carry him to where the cupboard is and tug one of the plastic sacks over his feet and legs and one over his head and his torso and prop him up in the cupboard and close the door on him. Unless they decide to take out the cupboard in the morning he'll be safe there till after Christmas.

I climb out of the corridor. Peter is still standing on the edge and he waits for me to walk past him and falls into step behind me.

When we get back to the car I get in the driving seat and Peter gets in the other side and when he's closed the door I say to him, "The only reason you're not propped up next to Eddie is because I couldn't carry the two of you on my own." He takes out one of his cheroots and tries to find his lighter.

"So you know what you're doing for Christmas, don't you?" I say to him.

He manages to light his cheroot but it takes him two or three goes. He blows the smoke out. "I was right," he says. "You know I was only talking sense back there."

"Yes and look where your sense got us."

He's quiet for a while.

"So what now?" he says at last.

"You're the one with all the bright ideas," I tell him. "I was hoping you'd tell me."

Mallory

BACK AT LESLEY'S FLAT. Con stands there open-mouthed while I tell him what happened when we went to see Eddie. When I've finished he looks at Peter.

"What's he doing still standing up?" he says. "Or have you saved him as your Christmas present from you to me?"

"That depends. I might decide to keep him myself. You know how it is with Christmas presents."

Con is still looking at Peter and Peter is avoiding that look by standing at the dresser and making himself a drink.

"So what the fuck do we do now?" Con says. "Go and ask Hume where Jimmy is? Seeing as it's Christmas, like. Because that's the only fucker left."

I take Eddie's address book out of my pocket and look through the addresses but nothing tells me anything I don't already know so finally I open it at the page headed APPOINTMENTS. Nice and neat, Eddie was, I think to myself, as I look down the entries written in small, boyish best-book handwriting. Must have got good marks from his teacher. But nothing could have warmed the cockles of his teacher's heart more than the last entry in the right-hand column. All it says is M. WATERLOO. And as I look at the initial and the word I remember the book open on the windowsill and some of the things that Eddie said while we were waiting for him to come off the phone, and in particular that yes, he'd be there at seven-thirty, no trouble, and yes, he'd bring it along. I close the book and think of the initial M. and look at the shiny black case lying like a square black diamond on top of the glass table. Then I get up and pour myself a drink and look at the case again.

"So how long do we wait here?" Con asks me. "I mean, I know we're on a hiding to nothing but I don't fancy lying down on my back with my legs in the air like a naughty dog."

I look at my watch. It's almost seven. I go over to the phone and dial Danny's number. Con swears and turns to the drinks and the dialing tone rings twice and then Audrey picks up the receiver at the other end.

"Have you done what I asked?"

"Yes," she says. "The boxes are at my flat."

"And?"

"There's almost thirty-five thousand."

I think about that for a minute or two and then I say, "All right, so put fifteen of it in a case and either Con or Peter'll be round to collect it in about half an hour."

"What for, for Christ's sake?"

"I might just need it," I tell her. "There's something come up but if that blows then the only thing I can do is try to use the money."

There is a short silence.

"All right," she says at last. "But—"

"No buts. Just do it. Just go back to the flat and do as I've said."

"And then what happens?"

"Depends. You made the other arrangements?"

"Yes. We can be on our way to Ireland at half an hour's notice. And while we're on our way he'll be fixing up the second leg."

"Right. So just do as I've said and wait for me to get in touch."

"How long will that be?"

"Christ knows," I say, and put the phone down and the minute I do that Con says, "Look, don't you think it's time we got well out of it? Christ, everything's fucked up now. So why are we hanging about?"

"You're not hanging about," I tell him. "You're going straight over to Gerald's flat and picking up a suitcase and bringing it straight back here. It shouldn't take you any longer than three-quarters of an hour."

"Fucking marvelous, isn't it?" Peter says. "I get a walloping for trying to sort out my own corner and now he's getting us to fetch and carry so he can get out himself."

I go over to Peter and brace him.

"Listen, you mug," I tell him, "when I decide to get out of it you'll be the first to know. Because I wouldn't leave until I'd seen to you."

Peter backs off and turns round and makes himself another drink.

Con puts on his coat and while he's fastening the buttons he indicates Peter and says, "Do I have to take him with me?"

"No, he's got to stay here and look after the girl. She still in the bedroom?"

Con nods and I go over to the bedroom door and open it and the smell that sweeps into my nostrils makes me think of the last time I smelt this particular smell, last night at the club when the spade stripper was up in the clouds. And now Lesley is that way too, half sitting, half lying on the bed, her back propped up against the wall at the top end of the bed. Smoke drifts idly round her while she stares straight ahead at her reflection in the two-way mirror. I look at her for a minute or two and she takes no notice of me whatsoever.

I close the door again and say to Peter, "You hear what I said?"

Peter moves his head slightly to show he heard me.

"The idea is that both you and the girl should be here when I get back. Right?" Peter nods again. I take the black case off the table just in case Peter should open it and get about twenty thousand ideas.

"I shan't be long," I tell him. "Remember what I told you earlier, at Eddie's."

"How could I ever forget?" he says.

• • •

I walk up the steps of the redesigned bar on Waterloo Station. It's all carpets and ice if you want it and soft lighting and smart colours but it still hasn't lost any of the British Rail tradition; it still manages to give the impression of dirt and unemptied ashtrays and tat. It always will, whatever they do.

I buy a drink and go and stand in the full-length plate-glass bowed window that juts out over the passing throng below. The tannoy system is impressing the Christmas spirit on the crowds by dribbling out "God Rest Ye Merry Gentlemen" but judging by the expressions on the faces, the music is wasted. The closest to the togetherness of Christmas this crowd will get is with one shared thought: why doesn't every other fucker get out of the way?

But I'm only interested in one probable member of that crowd, a member yet to join it and from where I am I'll have a perfect view as I look down at the back of the bookstall at the people meandering through from one side of the stall to the other.

I look at my watch. In five minutes he should be there, sweating for Eddie's arrival, looking round him like a child who's lost his mother. I light a cigarette and keep my eyes on the bookstall and in a moment or two he rounds the corner and looks all about him, searching for Eddie. I put my glass down and turn away from the window and walk towards the stairs.

When I get through the swing doors I go off at a tangent to the bookstall and make for the platforms. Then I make an about turn and approach the bookstall from the blind side and pass through the open part and push past the browsers and then I'm at the other side and almost directly behind Mallory, so close that he couldn't miss seeing me if he were to turn round. Which is what he does.

The features of Mallory's fat face seem to slip as if the skull beyond the flesh has turned to powder leaving nothing to support an expression. I get to him straight away and put a grip on him and immediately start walking away from the bookstand.

Mallory's a big man and though he's not as big as I am he would be difficult to shift if he didn't want shifting but now he's as limp as a bowl of tripe and he doesn't even realise he's moving and as we walk I say to him, "Come for your Christmas box, have you, Derek?"

Involuntarily he holds the briefcase he's carrying to his chest and with my free hand I take it from him and we walk off the station and past the taxis and round the corner to where I've parked the car. All the while we're walking Mallory doesn't say a word and he doesn't take his eyes off my face, as if I'm somebody he's known a long time ago and is desperately trying to recognise. I open the passenger door and guide him in and close the door on him and then I walk round to the other side of the car and get in myself.

I light a cigarette and when I've done that I say to him, "I can't understand you, Derek. I really can't. I mean, it isn't as though you weren't on a good screw, was it? I mean, you can't say you've not been looked after, can you?"

Mallory is still looking at me as if I'm Marley's ghost. His mouth opens and closes but no words come out. There is just the sound of the air from his lungs rattling the phlegm at the back of his throat.

"What can they do for you that we couldn't?" I ask him. "I mean, what more could they fucking well do? It's not the money, so what? Provide more birds that'll let you pump them up while you're wearing their knickers on your head? Do me a favour. Nobody could have looked after you better, not that way. No, it couldn't be that."

Mallory's mouth begins to open again but before he can complete the action I smash him so hard that his head bounces off the window and he finishes up with his face on my shoulder.

I push him away and take hold of him by the throat and I say into his face, "You fucking chancer. You fucking poxy chancer. You nearly fucking done the lot of us, didn't you?"

I let go of him and sit back in my seat and draw on my cigarette and look out of the window at the snowy scene. Mallory puts his hands to his face and leans his head against the dashboard. Eventually sounds begin to issue from between his fingers and I realise he's trying to talk to me.

"No choice," he's saying. "No choice. They made it quite clear, quite clear what would happen if I didn't. My wife, children. You understand that, of course you do."

"All I understand is what's happened during the last twenty-four hours," I tell him. "That's all I understand."

"I . . . "

"And all I want to know now is where Jimmy's being kept. The rest you can keep to your fucking self."

He shakes his head. "I don't know that," he says.

"Oh, yes."

He lifts his head from his hands and looks at me.

"Honestly," he says. "I don't know. I'd tell you, I really would."

"Don't worry," I say, starting the car. "You'll tell me all right. No fucking danger."

I put the car into gear.

While we're driving back to Crawford Street, Mallory keeps telling me how he'd got no choice and how he doesn't know where Jimmy is and I just let him get on with it and it occurs to me that for a lawyer he seems to have a very limited vocabulary.

Then eventually he gives up and the closer we get to Crawford Street, the more Mallory seems to take notice of the surroundings and at one point he says, "Where are we going?"

"Does it matter?" I say to him. "Does it really fucking matter, Derek?"

I park the car a way down the road from where the flat is and before we get out I say to Mallory, "Now you know as well as I do that there isn't any point in trying to make a break, even if you'd got the legs for it, because you know all that would achieve would be to make me irritated and you don't want that, do you?"

Mallory shakes his head and so I pick the black case off the back seat and get out and lock the door and walk round and let Mallory out the other side.

While we're walking along, I notice Mallory glancing at the black case.

"Not really worth it, was it, Derek," I say to him. "Not really worth it at all. Twenty grand? Jesus."

We're getting close to the corner where Lesley's block is and the closer we get the more difficult it seems to be for Mallory to put one foot in front of the other.

"Come on, Derek," I say to him. "Gee up. Not much further now."

We round the corner of the pub and get to the stairs and begin to climb them. I ring the bell. The sound echoes up and down the empty stairwell. I lean against the wall and look at Mallory. Under the yellow light his face looks more like a dead fish than ever.

I wait a minute or two and then I ring the bell again. There is no sound from behind the door. I ring the bell a third time and while I'm doing that I hear footsteps as someone down below turns in from the street. The footsteps stop and I take my finger off the bell and grab Mallory by the arm and shove him away from the door and up onto the next flight of stairs. I take my shooter from its holster and listen for the footsteps to start again. When they do they're very soft, very slow, and I listen to whoever it is stop when they're far enough up the stairs to see that there's no one outside the door to the flat.

And precisely at that moment the door to the flat opens and I hear Peter's voice say, "What the fuck are you playing at?"

And then I hear Con's voice answer, "Who rang the bell?"

And then I step into view and say, "Bang!"

Con is a few steps from the top of the flight of stairs. In one hand he is carrying the case he's just picked up from Audrey and in the other he is holding his shooter. Peter is framed in the doorway. He's not wearing his jacket and one of his cuffs is hanging loose and, for him, his hair is a mess and sweat is shining on his forehead.

"Jesus," Con says.

"No," I say. "There's two days to go till then."

I lean back and take Mallory's arm again and draw him into sight of Con and Peter.

"But maybe you can make do with this."

They both stare at Mallory and then a great smile breaks out on Con's face.

"Well," he says. "The George Best of the legal profession. Nice to see you again, Mr. Mallory."

Peter turns away and goes into the flat and I tell Con to bring in Mallory and I follow Peter through because I want to find out what's going on.

Peter is at the dresser, making himself another drink and the bottle is rattling slightly on the rim of the glass.

"She still in the bedroom?" I ask him.

He nods but he doesn't look round from what he's doing.

I begin to go over to the bedroom door and Peter says, "Well, she tried to get well out of it, didn't she?"

I stop walking towards the bedroom door and I turn round to look at Peter.

"You what?"

"She tried it on, didn't she? Said she wanted to go to the karsi. So I follow her out into the hall and she goes into the bathroom and I tell her to leave the door open but I don't get a chance to make sure it stays open because as soon as she's through it she slams it and throws the bleeding bolt, doesn't she? So I give the door a kicking and it gives but by that time she's standing on the karsi seat and halfway out the flaming window. And there isn't no flaming fire escape, is there? I mean, that would have been right handy, wouldn't it, her all over the back yard? So I pull her in and start to show her the error of her ways but she gives me a push and I lose my footing and fall in the bleeding bath and by the time I get out of it she's down the hall and out the front door. She's almost on the street by the time I get to her. So then I bring her back up here and by that time I'm well pleased. I mean, you can imagine."

Con and Mallory are now standing behind me, at the corner of the screen.

"Yes, I can imagine," I say quietly. "And then what did you do, Peter?"

Peter takes a sip of his drink and then looks at us all in turn, looking for a reflection of his reason.

"Well, I gave her a seeing to, didn't I?" he says. "Same as anybody would."

I look at him for a few moments. Then I turn away and walk over to the bedroom door and open it and the minute I open it there is a broken sound that is hardly loud enough to be called a sob.

At first I can't see her. Then I hear the sound again and I realise it's coming from the far side of the room, beyond the bed. I walk round the bed end and Lesley is lying on the floor between the side of the bed and the wall. She has her face buried in the remains of her sweater. There are three or four bruises on her back but that is nothing to what I find when I turn her over. Her bottom lip is split completely and three of her top teeth are missing. One side of her face is the colour of charcoal and will soon be turning deep purple. She draws her knees up to her chest and tries to turn back to the position she was in before. I let go of her and stand up. Con is standing behind me and he looks down at the girl for a moment then he turns round and strides for the bedroom door. I hurry after him but I'm not quick enough to stop him taking hold of Peter and start putting a few on him. I drag Con off him and stand between the two of them.

"There's no time," I say to Con. "If there was time for that he wouldn't have come back from Eddie's."

It takes a minute or two but finally Con manages to relax himself. I turn to Peter who by now is looking at his reflection in the long dark window and straightening himself up.

"Fucking bog Irish," he says. "What about a few choruses of 'Mother McChree?'"

I shake my head and as I do that there's a scream from the bedroom and I go through and see Mallory standing at the end of the bed and instead of Lesley being curled up face down she is shuffling herself across the carpet and into the corner and staring at Mallory as if he's about to take up where Peter left off. Mallory stoops down and stretches out a hand but she screams again and wriggles like a spitted eel and Mallory pulls his hand back as if he's just been burned.

He straightens up and away from her and looks into my face and says, "Did it have to take that much?"

I don't answer him.

"Or did you need the practice?"

"Getting brave in your old age, aren't you, Derek?" I say to him. "And believe me, it is your old age."

Mallory sits down on the end of the bed and at the same time Con comes into the room carrying a sponge and a towel.

"A good-looking piece like that," he says to himself as he crosses the bedroom to where Lesley is. Mallory also seems to be talking to himself.

"She must have given you the lot before you got that far," he's saying. "There was no reason for her not to. No reason. She'd already got what she'd been offered."

Con is now kneeling next to Lesley and beginning to go to work on her like a trainer and although she's staring at him the way she stared at Mallory she seems to be accepting Con's ministering. But my observation of this touching scene is beside the point. What I'm concentrating on are the words that are coming out of Mallory's mouth.

"Hang on," I say to Mallory. "What are you going on about? Peter gave her the seeing to."

"Of course," Mallory says. "That's why he's here."

"She tried to get out of it. You heard what happened."

Mallory's hearing seems to start functioning again.

"What?" he says.

"The girl made a break. Peter brought her back."

Mallory looks at me and I look at him and I get the weird feeling that Mallory's expression is a precise mirror image of my own because his jaw is low with disbelief and his eyes are reflecting my own furious concentration.

I walk over to him and sit next to him on the bed and take hold of the front of his coat.

"Now then," I say to him. "What are you talking about?"

He starts to shake his head and I start to shake the rest of him.

"What she was offered," I say to him. "What the fuck are you talking about?"

Mallory raises his arms and gently places his hands on mine and the way he does it causes me to stop shaking him and let go. Beyond his shoulder I can see that although Con is still dabbing away at Lesley's face he's focusing his concentration on Mallory and myself. Mallory passes a hand across his eyes and then slowly heaves himself up off the bed and walks out of the bedroom and then comes back carrying his briefcase. He stops in front of me and opens the case and takes out a Manila file tied up with crimson ribbon. He puts the case down on the bed and unties the crimson ribbon and riffles through the file until he finds a small white letter-size envelope. He looks at it for a moment and then he throws it onto the bed. I stretch out my hand and pick up the envelope. It isn't sealed so I flick open the flap and take out the contents of the envelope.

There are about a dozen postcard-size photographs and a cellophane packet containing some negatives. I look at the photographs. They are photographs of a man and a woman and they are doing all sorts of imaginative things to one another. For instance, in one photograph the girl is lying on a bed and has her wrists handcuffed together and the man, still fully dressed, is taking her clothes off, but not in the usual way; the clothes are being torn to shreds. Perhaps the man in the photograph is in a hurry. In another of the photographs the man is pushing the girl's face down into the quilt and in his free hand he is holding a thin cane with which he is beating the girl's bottom. And in another photograph the girl is kneeling on the floor, her hands now cuffed behind her back, and the man is sitting on the bed and grasping bunches of the girl's hair and pulling her down on him. The photographs are literally six of one and half a dozen of the other because half of them involve a reversal of roles in which the girl has the cane and the man is wearing the handcuffs and it is the girl who is pulling off the man's clothes, not tearing them, of course, because the suit is an expensive one and the shirt is handmade. And as I go through the photographs I am struck by my familiarity with the man and the woman and with their surroundings. Which is not surprising, as the bed I'm sitting on features prominently in most of the photographs and the girl is at present having her face repaired by Con McCarty.

Mallory sits down beside me on the bed.

"Walter's insurance," he says. "They had me set it up. The girl, this place. Everything."

Con stands up and walks round to our side of the bed.

"What's going on?" he says.

I look up at Con and then I hand him the photographs. He glances at the first one and then his eyelids flicker and he looks at me for a moment then moves on to the next photograph.

Mallory says, "You know what Walter's like. He wanted to have the edge. He was going to let him see the prints after Christmas, to let him know there was never any point in crossing Walter and Eddie at a later date."

While Mallory's talking Con begins to laugh, quietly at first, but the further he gets through the photographs the louder his laugh becomes and his laughter attracts Peter who appears in the doorway, holding his drink. Con continues laughing and Peter drifts over from the doorway and looks over Con's shoulder and then, like Con did, he shoots a quick glance at me and then maneuvers himself into a better position to see the photographs. Eventually Con stops laughing long enough for him to get some words out.

"Jesus Christ," he says. "What was it I said the other night? You can walk on the water?"

"I don't get it," Peter says, taking the pictures from Con. "This is—"

"We know," I tell him. "We fucking know."

"Jack the fucking Lad. All the time we've been charging all over the place and it was here. Right here."

"We didn't know that, did we?"

"Oh no, we didn't know that, did we. But you're Jack Carter, aren't you? And Jack Carter knows every fucking think there is to know, doesn't he? Or so he's always saying."

"Shut it."

"And the other thing, what was it? We'll be safe here. He won't be back. Supposing he'd come back for another session? Jesus fucking Christ."

"All right. I know. Now shut it."

"Supposing she'd shopped us? Supposing she'd given us to him?"

"Well, she didn't get the chance, did she? And besides, she didn't know what was going on. She'd no reason to connect us with him."

I get up off the bed and go out of the bedroom and start making myself a drink. Con follows me out.

"I mean, this is really one for the *Guinness Book of Records*, this one. Jack the Lad. Shacked up with all we need to sort the situation and he doesn't fucking know it."

I take a sip of my drink.

"Well, we know now, don't we?" I say.

Peter comes out of the bedroom, still looking at the photographs.

"I don't get it," he says. "What's Hume doing with this slag?"

Hume

I DRIVE ROUND AND round the island where the tube station is and after the second time I see Hume standing near the newsstand and after the fifth time I'm sure Hume has stuck to the conditions so I slow down and pull in to the curb, not quite coming to a standstill, and almost immediately Hume steps forward and opens the door and gets in and I pull away from the curb. I cross into the outer ring of traffic and take the first left and then some more lefts until I'm back on the roundabout again and this time my left turn is exactly opposite to the first one I took. Neither of us says anything to each other. Hume takes out his cigarettes and lights one up and I light up one of my own and I carry on driving until we've almost finished our cigarettes and then I pull into a side street just behind the Earls Court Road and park underneath the light of a streetlamp. After I've switched off the ignition I roll my window down and throw out my cigarette.

We sit there in silence for a few minutes and then Hume says, "So what's your deal?"

"My deal?" I say, all innocent, looking forward to the next five minutes.

"Don't shoot shit," Hume says. "You call me up and tell me you can give me the Fletchers, so you want to make a deal. You want me to leave you out of it. And while I'm lifting Gerald and Les you're over the sea to Skye."

I don't say anything.

"You make me sick," he says. "All you fucking heroes. Underneath it all you're all the fucking same."

"I suppose you're right, Mr. Hume," I say.

"Don't come it," he says. "You're in no position to give me that kind of crap."

I don't say anything.

"I really want the Fletchers," he says. "Lifting them will do me no end of good. But the thing is I'd like to take you just as much. Only you're not quite so famous as the other two. That's the only reason I'm even considering your scabby little deal."

"I realise that," I say, lighting up another cigarette. Then, almost as an afterthought, I say, "Oh, by the way. Eddie Coleman asked me to give you his Christmas card."

I take the envelope containing a single photograph out of my inside pocket and hold it out to him, not looking at him, as if I'm doing just what I described: delivering a Christmas card.

Hume is as motionless as a block of ice.

"Yes," I say. "I saw Eddie earlier. Said if you liked the card he'd let you have some more of the same so's you could send them round to your friends."

Hume still doesn't say anything but he reaches out and takes the envelope from me and looks at it without opening it.

"What is this?" Hume says at last.

I shrug. "Why not have a look and find out?"

Hume suddenly jerks to life and rips the envelope off the photograph and holds it at an angle to catch the light from the street-lamp and then when he's finally managed to believe his eyes he keeps staring at the picture as if in some way his staring will change what he sees in front of him.

"I thought the handcuffs were a nice touch," I say to him. "Special issue, were they?"

Hume makes a noise like a mad elephant and starts going to work on the photograph, not able to decide whether to crumble the picture or tear it to bits and his fingers alternate madly between the two actions. When he's finished he lets the remains of the photograph drop to the floor of the car.

"What you should never do," I tell him, "is do deals with villains. They just can't be trusted. You take my word for it."

Hume clenches his fist and hits himself on the forehead, just twice.

"Those cunts," he says. "Those fucking bastards."

"You really should have smelt it," I tell him. "I mean, a bird like that. A place like that. A man of your experience."

"Those fucking chancers. I had it made. With what Jimmy was going to put out I could have had twenty of you in the fucking dock. I'd have had more space than Reid."

"Yes, well, don't be like that. Look at it this way: I'm saving you a lot of bother. Instead of Walter having the snaps, we've got them. And me and Gerald and Les are much more reasonable to deal with than Walter. We wouldn't use them as a lever the way Walter would have. I mean, we'll *never* use them. We're much too nice for that."

There is silence for a while.

"All right," Hume says. "Tell me."

"You know what I want. And Jimmy apart, there are some events that have happened during the last twenty-four hours that you'll be laying at the door of the Colemans and one or two other people you won't find it hard to fit up. I mean, fitting people up is no new game to you, is it?"

"And if I tell you where to find Jimmy?"

"We'll smack his hands for him, won't we?"

"He's guarded day and night."

"'Course he is."

"You'll never manage it."

"Don't you worry about that. Think of all the other things you've got to worry about. Like what would happen if the pictures went to the Commissioner and the press. Think of all the fun you'd have thinking up your explanation."

"What about the Colemans? If I try to pull them they'll blow the whistle on me."

I shake my head.

"This time tomorrow they won't be in a position to blow the whistle on anybody. Ask Eddie. And so anything that happens from now on you can put down to them."

There is another silence.

After a while Hume says, "Jesus Christ."

And then, after he's said that, he begins to tell me what I want to know.

Jimmy

WHEN I GET BACK to the flat Peter is lying on the chaise longue reading a copy of *Vogue*. Mallory is on the other side of the screen sitting bolt upright on one of the Swedish chairs, his briefcase lying neatly on his lap. As I appear in the doorway Peter drops the magazine and sits up but Mallory stays the way he is, motionless, vacant.

"What happened?" Peter says.

I walk through the lounge and open the bedroom door. Lesley is now in bed, propped up with two pillows at her back. Con has wound a damp towel round her head and has cleaned up Lesley's mouth and he is now sitting on the edge of the bed, talking to her. They are both smoking and although Lesley's face isn't going to be straight for the next three weeks and in the meantime she's going to need a good dentist, she's better than she seemed earlier, both physically and mentally. Con looks up immediately I appear in the doorway and then I have both him and Peter asking me what happened with Hume. I turn away and push past Peter and pick up Eddie's black case from the tabletop and take it into the bedroom and motion for Con to get off the bed, and then for both him and Peter to go out of the room while I talk to Lesley. When they've closed the door behind them I sit down on the bed and put the case between Lesley and me and open up the lid. She looks at the money but it doesn't seem to do an awful lot to brighten up her expression.

I light a cigarette and I say, "It isn't that I think there's any danger of you going to the law, but there's one or two things I want to tell you, just in case. First, I know you only know what you were asked to do. Why should you know any more? You were fixed to set Hume up and you were paid for it. But what you will realise is that having done what you've done, you won't be all that popular if you go in to see them with your story. But by the same token, things having worked out a certain way, nobody'll be coming to see you either. From any direction."

She doesn't say anything. She's stopped staring at the money and now she's looking at me but her expression is still the same.

"And if nothing I've just said does anything for you, there's twenty thousand Christmas presents in the case that for a start will buy you a little sunshine to convalesce in."

She doesn't say anything for a minute or two. We carry on looking at each other.

Then she says, "I might prefer chancing the law. Seeing you and those others done might make me get well sooner."

Her voice is without expression and because of what's happened to her mouth she sounds like a different person.

"But we won't, not now. That's the point. You'd be turning the money down for nothing."

"Only on your say-so."

I shrug.

"And if you're telling me the truth, why the money? You don't need to do that."

"Walter didn't need to set up Hume. But he did. Everybody likes a little insurance."

"I could take the money and still drop you in it."

"Well, look at it this way," I tell her. "If you did, we'd know you were the only person who could."

An expression of remembered pain pulls briefly at her features. She doesn't say anything else after that.

I get up off the bed and stub out my cigarette in the ashtray on the bedside table and walk out into the lounge and close the door behind me. Con and Peter are standing there with their mouths open, like when West Germany knocked England out of the World Cup in Mexico. I go to the dresser and pour myself a drink.

"Oh, for fuck's sake," Con says. "What's happening?"

"We're going to wish Jimmy Swann a Merry Christmas," I say. "But first we've got to pick up one or two things along the way."

I put my drink down by the telephone and before they can start asking the whys and wherefores I've got Sammy Hale on the phone and at first, until he's convinced who's calling, he's understandably cagey, which is one of the things he's paid to be. I tell him what we want and that we'll be over inside the hour to pick the stuff up and he tells me it'll be ready. I put the phone down and the gabble starts again but I quieten them down by telling them I'll explain in the car. Then I put my hand on Mallory's shoulder and shake him out of his trance and tell him that it's time to go. Mallory raises his head and looks into my face as if that helps him to understand what I'm saying to him. Eventually he rises and I shepherd him across the lounge and out of the flat and Con and Peter follow and we go down the stairs and out into the street. I tell Peter where I'm parked and to go and get Lesley's Mini and follow us to Sammy's. This brings more abuse from Peter but I remind him of our earlier conversations and he goes off to get the Mini while Mallory and Con and I walk down to where the other car is parked. Con and Mallory get in the back and I get in the driver's seat and switch on the engine and we wait for Lesley's Mini to appear. I look at my watch. The atmosphere in the car is thick with Mallory's fear. It's like waiting for a drip of water to fall from the mouth of a tap; any second I expect Mallory to blow it, for the words to come streaming out, but they don't, not until the very last minute, when I see the flashing of Peter's headlights in my driving mirror, and then it all comes out, a stream of consciousness as inventive as the "One-Note Samba," running together into one long plea for his life. I tell him to shut up and pull away from the curb but he doesn't stop and for the next five minutes we're treated to descriptions of Mallory's wife and children and their lives without him, when of course Mallory is only thinking of his life without himself.

After a while I can't stand it any longer so I pull in to the curb and say to Con, "All right. Let the cunt out."

Mallory stops in midstream.

"You what?" Con says.

"Let him out."

"You're joking."

"All right, I'm joking. So let him out."

In the driving mirror I see the lights of the Mini as Peter pulls in behind us. Con begins to speak again but I cut him short.

"So what can he do? Go to the law?"

Con digests that and then leans across Mallory and opens the nearside door. The door swings open but Mallory doesn't move. In the mirror I can see Peter get out of the Mini and walk along the pavement towards us.

Still Mallory remains where he is so I turn round in my seat and I say to him, "Look, just get out of it, will you? If Gerald and Les want you put down I'll come looking for you in the New Year. Until then it's up to you. So just piss off, will you, before I start remembering how this whole fucking shambles started."

Peter appears at the open door and bends down and sticks his head inside the car.

"You're not doing it here?" he says.

"Piss off," I say.

"He's letting him go," Con says.

"What?" Peter says.

I look at Peter. Peter steps back and straightens up.

"Jesus fucking Christ," he says.

"Out," I say to Mallory.

Mallory suddenly jerks to life and slithers out of the car. Peter braces him and then feints like a striker trying to sell a defender a dummy and Mallory falls back against the car and rolls against it a couple of times, his briefcase banging on the roof and then he manages to coordinate his legs and takes off down the street, the snow lending an odd softness to the fury of his retreating footsteps.

Peter mentions Jesus again and spits into the snow and turns away and walks back to the Mini. Con slams the door and I pull away from the curb and drive off down the street. We pass Mallory on the way, oblivious of the car, sprinting through the falling snow, focusing only on the unexpected years he now has in front of him.

Ten minutes later we're in Hammersmith. I park outside Sammy's place. Con and I get out of the car and go up the steps and ring the doorbell. Almost immediately Sammy opens the door and just as quickly closes it behind us. We negotiate the pram and bicycle in the hall and Sammy ushers us into his flat. Rachmann would have loved it, but Sammy prefers money to wallpaper. His fat wife is watching the colour telly, the only visible proof of the money he's being paid. As for the rest of the flat, it's the kind of place you try very hard not to notice while you're in it and to forget after you've gone. Sammy indicates the table. A dirty tablecloth is draped over the objects that Sammy has laid out for us before we've arrived, only underneath we're not going to find a nicely set out tea party. The doorbell rings and I tell Sammy to go and let Peter in. Sammy's old lady takes no notice of us and carries on watching the telly. She doesn't even move when, from behind the concertinaed paneling that divides the flat into two, comes the sound of a crying baby.

I peel back the tablecloth. Con and I look at the stuff that Sammy has laid out for us and while we're doing that

Peter comes into the room and pushes between us and has a look at the tabletop. A great smile spreads over his face.

"Oh, favourite," he says. "Fucking favourite."

I stand to one side so he can get a better view and as I do that I notice that Peter is carrying a shiny black case, a case that I last saw twenty minutes ago, lying on Lesley's bed. Con happens to catch my eye and follows my line of vision to what I'm looking at. Then he looks back at me and closes his eyes and shakes his head. But Peter only has eyes for what's on the tabletop.

"Oh, yes," he says. "The fucking berries, that's what this is. The fucking berries."

He puts the case down and reaches over the table and picks up the rifle with the telescopic sights and starts handling it as though he's playing with himself. I pick up the case and open it and close it again. The twenty thousand is still there. The baby is still crying and Sammy's old lady is still doing nothing about it.

Con has opened his eyes again and I stare into them and then I say to Peter, "Tell me about it."

Peter is still drooling over the rifle.

"What?" he says, not really having heard me.

I tap the case. "Tell me about this."

Peter glances at the case.

"Oh, that," he says, turning his attention back to the rifle. "Favourite, isn't it? Gerald and Les'll like me for that part."

"What part is that, Peter?" I ask him.

Peter snaps back from his private paradise.

"Oh, do me a fucking favour," he says. "What you trying to come? I've done *you* a fucking favour. I've done Gerald and Les a fucking favour. What is this, the Gang Show? I've saved Gerald and Les more than just twenty grand. Fucking stroll-on. I mean, you didn't have the balls for it, did you? Fucking right you didn't. And then Mallory. Jesus fucking wept."

I'm about to do what I've been wanting to do for the last twenty-four hours but now it's Con's turn to stand between me and Peter. He grips my wrists and pushes his face close to mine.

"No," he says. "Remember. Remember what you said to me, Jack. We haven't the time. Not this time. But there's always another time. Isn't there, Jack?"

I look into Con's face again and then I look beyond his shoulder and I see that Peter is back in his own private communion with the rifle. I relax myself and try to make my mind a blank by thinking forward to our call on Jimmy Swann but all there is in the front of my brain are the pictures of Lesley and Hume as they were in the photographs.

"All right, is it, Jack?" Sammy says to me. I turn to look at Sammy and Con releases his grip.

"It's all there," Sammy says. "Everything you asked for."

I can't speak right away so Con answers on my behalf.

"Yeah, it's great, Sammy. Everything's lovely. You'll be on extras for this."

"The other stuff I was lucky with," Sammy says. "The shooters were no problem. But the other stuff . . . "

"Yes, Sammy," I tell him. "Like Con says, you'll be on extras."

"I only . . . " Sammy says, but he doesn't finish the sentence. Instead he turns to his wife.

"Can't you shut that little bleeder's noise?"

"Shut it yourself," his old lady says, not even bothering to look at him.

"Anyway," I say to Sammy, "thanks again. Somebody'll be round after Christmas."

Sammy nods and Con and I begin to gather up the goods and put them in the cricket bag that Sammy has thoughtfully placed on a sofa for us. Con takes the rifle off Peter and puts it with the rest of the stock and then I pick up the cricket bag and we go out of the flat and into the hall and Sammy opens the front door for us.

As I go out I say to Sammy, "Well, thanks again, Sammy. As I say, we'll be in touch."

"Yeah. Fine."

He wishes us a Merry Christmas and we go down the steps to where the car Con and I came in is parked.

"Right," I say to Con and Peter. "Get in and I'll tell you the drill."

Peter gets in the back and Con gets in the passenger seat beside me.

After I've briefed them I ask them to tell me what I've just told them and they do, word perfect, and then I say, "The important thing, for both parties, is not the actual blast. It's making sure of the way out. I've already done it, but not in a hurry. Any panic, in the dark, and you're dead. Same applies to me. I've got the same kind of route, but if I run into a greenhouse or a trellis fence then I'm finished. But it's more important for Con than for me. Because the second it blows he's got to be out of it. And the car's got to be moving before he's in it. But not too quick, Peter, eh? He's got to get in it, right?"

I look at Peter but because of the darkness in the back of the car I can't tell whether or not he's made a gesture so I ask him again and he forces himself to answer.

"The point is," I say, "it's not so important for me to move quite so fast. They won't be expecting what's coming from me, and by the time they work out which direction it's come from I'll be in the other motor and off. But for Con, all they've got to do is look out onto the back garden and they could see him as clear as if he was strolling under Blackpool Illuminations. So try the way back first, before you do the plant."

"Too fucking right I'll try it first," Con says.

"It's the kitchen that'll get the blast. According to Hume, at that time of night there's a two on two off in the hall and those that are off doss down upstairs in Jimmy's room. His wife and kids are somewhere else. So unless someone comes into the kitchen to make a pot of tea, the kitchen will be dark and there'll be no light shining on the activities underneath the kitchen window."

"Oh, well," Con says. "That makes all the difference. I mean, I've got nothing to worry about, have I?"

"Just one small point," Peter says. "A detail, really. How is it you're the one with the safe job? How is it you're the one over the road?"

I look at his vague shape in the darkness. "You want to ask that question again?"

Peter doesn't ask the question again.

"Right," I say. "I'll take the Mini. You two use this. And afterwards I'll meet you where we arranged."

I open the door and get out and before I close it Con says, "What happens if it doesn't work?"

"Don't ask," I say, and close the door.

Half an hour later I'm parking the Mini in the street that runs parallel to the one where Jimmy's safe house is. I get out and push the driving seat forward and take the rifle out of the bag on the back seat and wrap it in my overcoat and close the door and cross the road.

Most of the houses are dark, and I'm glad the house I'm interested in isn't one of the exceptions. I go to the front gate and look around me and after I've done that I straddle the gate and walk over to the built-on garage and open the trellis gate and walk down the path that runs alongside the garage. I pause at the corner of the gate in case a light from the kitchen or the room above is illuminating the back garden but I'm in luck. So I cross the small lawn and pass the garden shed and climb over the low fence that separates this garden from the ones at the back of the houses that face on to the parallel street beyond. I cross the second garden and reach the other house and this one doesn't have a built-on garage so I walk along the path that runs along the side of the house and stop when I get to the corner. Then I have a look at Jimmy Swann's safe house, two houses down on the opposite side of the road. There is only one light shining out into the night and that is coming from the diamond window in the front door, illuminating the

For Sale sign in the front garden. The rest is dark as Jimmy Swann's grave.

I lean back against the wall and look at my watch. The illuminated dial tells me there's five minutes to go until Con does his party piece. I look up at the night sky. It's clear now, and all the stars are sharp and bright against the blackness. I take my cigarettes out and put one in my mouth without lighting it and suck on it now and then. I look at my watch again. A minute to go. I unwind my overcoat from round the rifle and then I put my overcoat on and have a look across the road. From the angle I'm at I can see the black shape of the smallest kitchen window set in the side of the house. Con should be under it by now but I can't make out any movement. By now he should have the air-brick well and truly filled and by now he should be setting the fuse. Either Con's getting good in his old age or he hasn't fucking well turned up. And then I see what I've been waiting for. A match is struck, the flame dies, and the sparks begin, but before the match goes out I can see the bent shape of Con legging it round to the back of the house. I settle the rifle into my shoulder and watch the sparks fizzing onto the hard dry snow. Then, behind me, an oblong of light flashes onto the wall of the next house and then after that there is the sound of a door opening and the clink of milk bottles. I turn round and see a doubled-up figure about to place the bottles on the step and my movement causes the figure, a man in a dressing gown, to incline its head in my direction and then straighten up and at that precise moment the explosion rocks the whole street and strangely enough the loudest sound in my ears seems to be the smashing of the dropped milk bottles behind me. I whirl round and look across the road and I'm just in time to see the whole of the back of the house lit up as Con hurls the petrol bombs through the big kitchen window round the other side. Frames explode from the small side window and I know from their size and their sound that

Con has done it just right. Upstairs the lights go on and down below I can see a faint glow begin to illuminate the front rooms' dark windows.

Then the front door flies open and a shirt-sleeved figure races round to the side of the house and from behind me the other figure says, "What the bloody hell . . . "

But before he can say any more I turn round and point the rifle at him and he half backs, half falls back into the house. I swing round again. By now the flames are beautiful. I can even see them billowing out from the blind side of the house. I put my eye to the sight and then I have the open front door in my vision, and through the door comes another piece of filth, dragging a shooter from a shoulder holster, not having any idea what he's going to do with it once he's got it out. And almost immediately after this figure come two more, and one of them is Jimmy Swann.

Jimmy is wearing a neat red satin dressing gown but there's nothing neat about his face, foreshortened and distorted in my sights; he looks like an astronaut experiencing twenty Gs. The filth who's shepherding him out is superfluous. Jimmy really doesn't need any guidance, and as he hurries down the garden path away from the flames, to safety, I steady the rifle so that the cross is resting perfectly on the middle of Jimmy's furrowed forehead, and then I pull the trigger three times, and immediately the last bullet leaves the barrel I turn away and run back down the side of the house, and as I pass the open door I glance into the house but there is no sign of the man who'd been putting out the milk bottles. That's the trouble with the world today, I reflect. A lack of public spirit. Nobody seems to be prepared to have a go these days.

Walter

DAWN.

The leaden sky soars above us, making the passing snowy fields seem twice as brilliant and even though we're traveling the broadness of the landscape gives the impression that we're not traveling fast at all.

Peter is asleep on the back seat and I'm sitting in front next to Con, my head resting on the back of the seat, eyes half closed, enjoying the irresponsible sensation of being driven by a good driver.

But I don't want to doze off again so I take my cigarettes out and light up and then I say to Con, "Ever fancied living out here, Con? I mean, in the country?"

"'Course I have, haven't I?" he says. "I mean, I don't just have the lockup. I got a nice little place between Saffron Walden and Thaxted."

"Yeah, the lockup," I say.

"Nice place," Con says. "Got in before the boom, didn't I? How I got on to it was, I figured the lockup might come in handy one day, so while I was scouting it I drove about a bit and I come across this place and I think to myself, Just the kind of place my old mother would have liked, if she'd have lived to see it. Roses round the door and all that. So I bought it. Four grand it cost me. Fucking criminal."

I sit up and take the map from the glove compartment, then I unfold the map and have a look and after I've done that I say to Con, "You should be at Otley in about ten minutes. You go through it and you keep straight on, making for a place called Cretingham, but you don't go as far as that. I'll tell you where to turn off."

In the back of the car Peter stirs and raises himself up on one elbow and looks out of the window as if he's looking at the surface of the moon.

"Where the fucking hell are we?" he says.

Neither of us answers him. He sits up properly and takes a small mirror out of his inside pocket and starts tarting himself up.

We drive through Otley, a long-strung-out village with a new estate on its outskirts, and then we find the road that leads to Cretingham and I take out Eddie's notebook and start looking for Blackbird Lane. A few minutes later I spot the signpost but Con is already past it so he brakes hard and reverses back past the turning.

"Take it slow from now on," I tell him.

"There doesn't seem to be a lot of choice," Con says, and I can see what he means. Blackbird Lane twists and turns and is only wide enough for one car at a time. There are lots of small muddy lay-bys so you can pull in if something's coming the other way. We drive along between deep hedges for about ten minutes and then we round a corner and we're on the brow of a hill and before us is a small valley, the road we're on twisting down into it and up the other side. I tell Con to stop the car. On the valley's opposite slope, there is a layout that could only belong to Walter Coleman. It's so neat and tidy that from where we are it looks like a child's model farm. It sticks out the same way an office block would in this rambling landscape. Everything's just been done up, the gates, the gardens, the footpaths. Even the barn roofs have been retiled. You can almost see the shine on the coaching lamps and count the pebbles on the newly laid drive.

"The Coleman estate," I say to Con.

"Makes my four thousand look silly," Con says.

Behind me, I hear some metallic sounds and I turn round to see Peter sorting a shotgun out of the cricket bag.

"What do you think you're playing at?" I say to him.

Peter looks at me as if I'm speaking a foreign language.

"You think we're going straight in, just like that?"

"We did with Jimmy," he says.

Con and I look at each other.

"We had no choice, did we?" I say to Peter. "This time we can play it the way we want it. I know you'd like to go in blasting but that's not the way it's going to be."

"What way is it going to be, then?" Peter says.

I take the field glasses from the glove compartment and focus them on Walter's farmhouse.

"You'll know when I tell you," I say to him, and then I say to Con, "There's a cart track about thirty yards back. Reverse the car and we'll leave it there."

Con slips it into reverse and we crawl back down the lane until we come to the track and then Con maneuvers the car into it and switches off the engine. I tell them to stay in the car and I go back to where the track and the lane meet and walk down the lane until I come to the brow of the hill and Walter's layout is once again in view. I look around me. This part of the hedgerow must belong to a different farmer because the hedges here have all been trimmed right down to the slopes of the ditches. Even the trees have been lopped off, and there is a snow-covered stump nearby so I jump the ditch and scramble up the far bank and dust off the snow and then sit down on the neat remains of the tree.

The gray sky is very still and its dullness accentuates the cleaned-up lines of Walter's property. There is a light on in an upstairs room and what I take to be the kitchen is also glowing out into the blue-gray day. There is some activity around the stables as Walter's local minions begin their daily round. Horses are led here and there, and Walter's BMW is slid out of the barn which has been converted into a garage and a member of staff begins to set about the motor with a handful of dusters. When he's satisfied with the outside he opens all four doors and takes a dustpan and brush to the inside. Then after that he gets into the driver's seat and does some very careful maneuvering until the BMW's in a position to be hooked up with a horse box standing close to the stables. After I've watched that fascinating operation I put the field glasses down and have a cigarette and look around me at the local countryside and enjoy it for a while. Then when I've finished my cigarette I walk back to the car. Peter is lying back smoking and Con is snoring in the passenger seat, his knees propped up against the dashboard. I bang on the side of the car with the flat of my hand and Con jackknifes forward and almost puts himself out against the windscreen.

I open the car door and say, "Your turn."

Con fucks and blinds and eases himself out of the car and as I get in I tell him to let me know when Walter shows himself. The car door slams and I sink back in the warm seat and almost immediately I begin to doze off but sleep won't come because in my mind I keep seeing Lesley in various attitudes of death, dead in a variety of ways. At one point I sit up and turn to face Peter, prepared to ask for the details of what happened, but when I look into his green cat-like eyes I decide against it and turn round and try to sleep again.

I seem to have been asleep for just five seconds when the car door opens and Con is standing there.

"Walter's come out to play," he says.

Peter and I get out of the car and all three of us run to the end of the track and down the road.

"Wait till you see him," Con says as we trot along. "He looks a treat."

We get to the brow of the hill and I take the glasses from Con and focus them on the farm. Walter is standing watching the stable boys coax his horse into the horse box. Con was right. He looks a proper treat. From the ribbon on his hard hat through the immaculate black jacket and the perfect jodhpurs and the shining black boots. When the horse is finally bolted in, Walter gets in his motor and negotiates the yard and drives slowly down the track that leads from his house to the road. He's obviously going to the meet without his old lady. Who wouldn't, with an old lady like Walter's? I watch his progress until he comes to the junction and then wait to see which way he's going to go. And then I see he's going to go left, which is fine, because that means he's coming in our direction. I turn away and start running back towards the car and Con and Peter follow after me. When I get to the car I slide into the driver's seat and switch on the ignition and start nosing the motor to the end of the track and Peter and Con get in as the motor moves along. I stop the car at the end of the track and wait to hear Walter's BMW swishing along the lane. I don't have to wait long. Con and Peter are already kitted out. Through the hedge I can see the metallic blue of Walter's motor. Then I put my foot down and Walter is confronted by the sight of our motor, and our three faces looking at him. I give him credit for his thinking because he slews his car across the lane so that the driving side is furthest away from us and he's out of his motor and off down the road like a rocket. But so are we, shouting and bawling after him like kids playing Tracking. Walter veers to the right of the lane and jumps the ditch and starts staggering across the frozen field to the cover of a small copse about twenty yards from the road. Peter and I jump the ditch after him but Con pauses on the road to try and get one in but Peter and I are in the line of fire and Con curses us and by that time Walter is in the trees. I swear as we get to the wood, but once in the trees I realise that Walter's not going to be hard to find because I hear him swearing and cursing himself, and a couple of yards in I can see the reason for his anguish. There is a small frozen pond directly in the chosen path of Walter's flight, hidden from view by banks of ground elder, and now Walter is waist-deep in the middle of that pond, his black coat stark against the grayness of the ice around, the ice he is trying to flail a path through to the other side.

"Walter," I call out.

Walter doesn't stop. He is mad with the need to reach the other side.

"You should learn your geography better," I tell him.

Walter overbalances and goes right under and when he comes up again he is facing our way. Peter is jumping up and down beside me. Walter's arms continue to flap at the jagged ice around him.

"You chancer," I tell him. "You fucking chancer. You took a dead fucking liberty."

But before I can tell him any more Peter is unable to hold back and both barrels of the shotgun he's holding boom out in the silence of the wood and Walter is lifted back as far to the other side as he'll ever get, and it doesn't matter anyway, because he no longer has a face.

Peter reloads and then we both watch Walter's body bobbing up and down on the rippling water, and the fragments of ice with the robin-redbreast blood spots swirling round him. Then we turn away and walk to the edge of the wood and find Con there, at the edge, waiting for us.

The three of us walk back across the icy field. The sky seems even grayer. Halfway across the field a pheasant flies up in front of us. Peter lets out a yell of delight and levels his shotgun but I put my hand on the barrels and push it down. Peter looks at me, dismayed.

"Leave it out," I tell him. "What do you want to do, get us done? They might be out of season."

• • •

I'm lying in bed, on my back, smoking. The dead Christmas Day afternoon fills the windows like lead. Outside, everything is quiet. The only sound I'm aware of is Audrey's light breathing as she lies sleeping beside me.

Then the phone rings. Audrey sits up, wide awake.

"Jesus Christ," she says.

"No," I say, reaching out, "it's just the telephone."

I pick up the receiver. An operator says, "Is that -----?"

"Yes," I say, because only three people have that number.

"I have an overseas call for you. Hold the line, please."

Audrey lies back in bed. A minute later Gerald's voice comes crackling down the line from Ibiza.

"Jack? That you? Listen, why the Christ haven't you been in touch? We've been waiting, what's—"

I cut him off. "Hello?" I say, as if I can't hear him. "Hello?"

"Christ," I hear him telling Les, "the fucking line's all to cock. Jack, listen, can you hear me? It's Gerald. Jack . . . "

"Hello?" I say again. "Hello?"

"For fuck's sake . . . "

"Whoever it is, I should call back on another line," I say, and then I put the receiver down and when it's been down long enough to cut them off I lift it again and leave it off the hook.

"Who was it?" Audrey asks.

"Santa's little helpers," I tell her. "They're going to have a lovely Christmas, now all the work has been done."

I look at my watch. "Nearly three o'clock," I say to Audrey. "Almost time for the Queen's Speech."

There is no response from Audrey.

"Still," I say, turning towards her, "there's always next year."

About the Author

Born in Manchester, England, Ted Lewis (1940–1982)
spent most of his youth in Barton-upon-Humber in the
north of England. After graduating from Hull Art School,
Lewis moved to London and first worked in advertising
before becoming an animation specialist, working on the
Beatles' *Yellow Submarine*. A pioneer of the British noir
school, Lewis authored nine novels, the second of which
was famously adapted in 1971 as the now iconic *Get Carter*,
which stars Michael Caine.

THE JACK CARTER TRILOGY

Meet Jack Carter, London's suavest fixer, before his trip north

GET CARTER

Famously adapted into the iconic film starring Michael Caine, Get Carter ranks among the most canonical of crime novels.

It's a rainy night in a northern English mill town, and a London fixer named Jack Carter is home for a funeral—his brother Frank's. Frank was very drunk when he drove his car off a cliff and that doesn't sit well with Jack. Mild-mannered Frank never touched the stuff.

Set in the late 1960s amidst the smokestacks and hardcases of the industrial north of England, *Get Carter* redefined British crime fiction and cinema alike. Along with the other two novels in the Jack Carter Trilogy, it is one of the most important crime novels of all time.

JACK CARTER AND THE MAFIA PIGEON

Published in North America for the first time—the final Jack Carter novel has London's slickest operator journeying to a Spanish villa to protect a wise-cracking Italian-American mobster.

Jack Carter is not thrilled when his frustratingly unprofessional employers—London mob kingpins Gerald and Les Fletcher—force him to take a vacation. Jack doesn't like leaving the business in other people's hands, but the company villa in Spain promises sunshine and some time to plot his next move.

Jack is surprised to find the villa inhabited by a cowardly house steward and a knuckle-dragging American gangster Jack has apparently been sent to protect the American, who has turned informant. There are few things that Jack Carter hates more than surprises. Informants being one of them.

SYNDICATE BOOKS

www.syndicatebooks.com